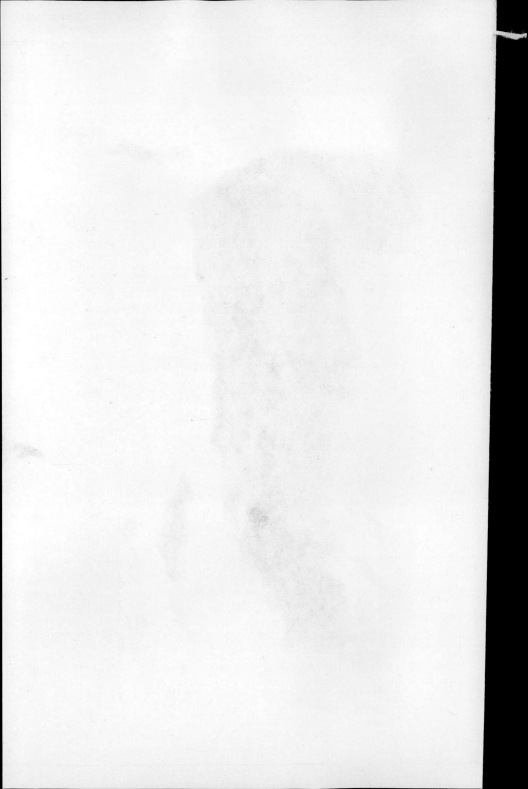

THE DIRTY WAR

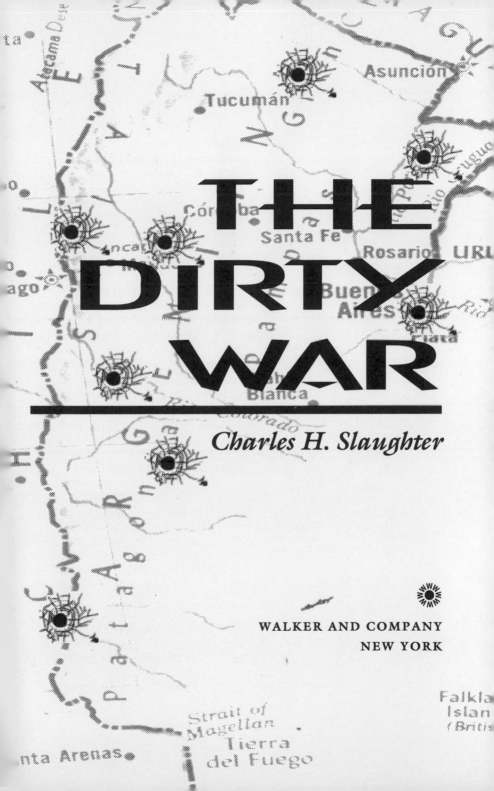

THE
DIRTY
WAR

Charles H. Slaughter

WALKER AND COMPANY

NEW YORK

Copyright © 1994 by Charles H. Slaughter

First published in the United States of America in 1994 by Walker Publishing Company, Inc.

Published simultaneously in Canada by Thomas Allen & Son Canada, Limited, Markham, Ontario

Library of Congress Cataloging-in-Publication Data
Slaughter, Charles H.
The Dirty War : a novel / by Charles H. Slaughter.
p. cm.
Summary: Argentina in 1976 becomes a frightening homeland for fourteen-year-old Atre and his family when the government takeover by the military results in the disappearance of thousands of innocent people.
ISBN 0-8027-8312-0
1. Argentina—History—1955–1983—Juvenile fiction.
[1. Argentina—History—1955–1983—Fiction. 2. Disappeared persons—Fiction.] I. Title.
PZ7.S6297Di 1994
[Fic]—dc20 94-4355
CIP
AC

BOOK DESIGN BY GLEN M. EDELSTEIN

Printed in the United States of America

1 2 3 4 5 6 7 8 9 10

Acknowledgments

I WISH TO EXPRESS MY SPECIAL APPRECIATION TO MR. Nicolas Tozer, editor of the *Buenos Aires Herald,* who opened his doors and provided a work desk for me. He gave valuable advice and support while my wife and I lived in Buenos Aires.

Senator Ricardo E. Laferrerie, of the Argentine Senate, provided significant help in developing key elements of the story. He was arrested during the Dirty War and held for a time.

Esmerelda Gómez, public information officer to Senator Laferrerie, was a student during the Dirty War and proved to be an exceptional resource. Her friendship added a special dimension to our time in Buenos Aires.

Mr. Robert Cox, a journalist's journalist, was editor of the *Buenos Aires Herald* during the time this story takes place. He was subjected to intense personal terrorism and is a recognized Argentine hero. Mr. Cox reviewed this manuscript.

And an additional note of respect and gratitude to the Mothers and Grandmothers of the Plaza de Mayo.

THE DIRTY WAR

1

5 MARCH 1976, BUENOS AIRES: Growing violence is putting pressure on President Isabel Perón to resign. Her chief congressional ally once again refused to call a joint session to deal directly with the violence and economic chaos. During yesterday's Brown Ceremony, civilian spectators applauded military dignitaries while virtually ignoring the Secretary of Defense. Public support for the incumbent government seems at an all-time low.

NOBODY CALLS CHINO HIS REAL NAME, ROBERT Echavarria, not since he was six and learning to draw. He kept drawing one picture, over and over, a Chinese man smoking a little pipe.

Chino has always been my best friend, ever since the first time Papá took me to La Barca Restaurant. We weren't yet five years old, and Señor Echavarria gave us a job folding napkins while he and Papá talked. We've been together ever since: playing, hanging out, getting in trouble. Like that morning at the Caminito.

We watched an army jeep screech past a sixty-passenger tourist bus and dart into the parking place marked *Reservado Turismo*. The bus driver shook his fist at the jeep. Instantly, the two soldiers in the backseat raised their rifles and flipped the bolts, loading rounds in the firing chambers. The bus driver cringed as he turned the bus to a vacant space in front of Gino's Barber Shop Café. The rifles dropped. It ended in a second; none of the passengers saw it.

Chino and me were standing by the bus stop. He was bug-eyed. "You see that?"

I saw it and had turned icy for a second, but I tried to ignore it. "So what? We have our own problem. Remember Horsey Zolezzi, the guy leaning against a power pole across the street?"

"Yes, but those soldiers weren't kidding. You ever see soldiers do that?"

It was scary. Soldiers had never before acted like that around our neighborhood. Besides, we had other things to worry about.

Chino and I ran an exclusive Caminito tourist business. Horsey thought just because he was a lot bigger than us he could move in. Well, we couldn't let that happen. Without the Caminito job, Chino had almost nothing. Me? I could either make my own money or ask my father. Some choice! So, the moment had finally come when we would all find out who would work the Caminito.

Bright noon sunlight bounced off the red bus. The long, gray side windows looked big enough to fit on a house. Rich-looking tourists stepped out slowly. Practically every nose gave a little twitch as it left the air-conditioned bus and took the first whiff of river smell that fills La Boca. Most looked a little nervous. Their eyes darted this way and that. The women turned their rings over to hide the stones while the men patted their jacket and hip pockets. When they caught sight of the artists' easels and paintings in the Caminito, they relaxed some.

As they moved onto the Caminito, I picked out a rich *jonnie* and his *señora*. She wore about a trillion pesos worth of jewelry.

"Stand beside me," I whispered. "When I start talking, you hold your foot so they can see the sole coming off your shoe."

"Atre? I am buying new shoes." Chino said my name slow and sad like I'd hurt his feelings: "Ahh-Trray."

"So, buy new shoes, just remember to wear those to work."

We went over to the couple like we always did. I spoke to the *jonnies* in English (that's what made our business work). I said, "*Señor, Señora*. Welcome to the Caminito. It is very safe for you here."

We held up our ID cards, and I kept talking. "My friend and I watch for the pickpockets while you look at the paintings. The artists hope you like their work and will take a painting home with you to remember your trip to Buenos Aires."

That's when the trouble started. Horsey butted in and messed it up.

His real name was Hector Zolezzi; he had a long face and a lot of extra forehead, like a cracker box standing on one end, what we call a *cara de caballo*, a horse face. That's why I named him Horsey. Told him Horsey is what people in the U.S. call their cowboys.

Horsey put his face right in front of the *jonnie*'s. *"Señor!"* he said, tapping his finger on his own chest as if he was something special. He reached back and pushed me away.

I grabbed Horsey's arm and spun him around.

"Beat it, Zolezzi! You scare the *jonnies*. They think you're a thief. Find your own street."

He doubled up his fist and drew his arm back. "Don't tell me to beat it." I held up both my hands and stepped away. Chino motioned the *jonnies* to come toward him, but they didn't move.

I kept my voice low. I didn't want that big *gorila* on me, and I didn't want the *turistas* to get upset.

We talked Spanish, naturally. Horsey had never learned English. I figured if I talked fast we could settle it in a hurry, without losing the customers.

Horsey got loud. "You *pendejos* scare *turistas* with lies about pickpockets. I got as much right to hustle them as you do."

"Put your hands down, Horsey. They think you're a mugger."

He dropped his hands and unclenched his fists. "I am not!"

He shouldn't have been there. He was sixteen, way too old for what we were doing. Fourteen is about as old as you can get and still have the right look. He should have known that, but he was a horse's ass. He screwed it up for anybody ever making any more money at the Caminito.

We were still arguing when the *jonnie* went to the corner and found Officer Bustamante, our local cop.

The *jonnie* had understood everything we said and repeated it to Busti. Not only that, but he mentioned our ID cards, something Bustamante didn't know about. As soon as I saw Busti's face, I knew we were in a lot more trouble than just arguing with Horsey Zolezzi.

Busti jammed his finger in Horsey's chest. "*You go home,* and stay there until I come and get you. I'll talk to your father later."

Señor Zolezzi, Horsey's father, was a pretty good guy, head of the La Boca Dockworkers Union, the UTP.

The Caminito is down by the docks, next to the big old Río Riachuelo bridge, in La Boca district of Buenos Aires. That's where we live. It's across the river from the slaughterhouses. Most people who live there work on boats, or the docks, or in meatpacking plants. It's a tough part of town, but a lot of tourists visit because it's colorful. La Boca houses are painted bright colors because boat owners paint them with leftover bottom paint. You see lots of deep red, blazing blue, and dark green houses.

The Caminito is one little street where artists set up easels and tables to show off their paintings. Chino said most of them weren't very good, but they made the Caminito special and tourists came. Our business was helping the tourists relax and enjoy themselves. In good times a lot of *turistas* came from the States and England. They almost never knew Spanish, and I know English. So, I talked to them, made them feel at home.

Tourists gave us "hard" money, mostly *yanqui* money from the States or *jonnie* money from England. Argentina money is no good since the inflation: A thousand pesos is worth less in the afternoon than it was in the morning. Hard money is worth the same every day. Two summers before we made lots of money, but since then business hadn't been so good. The *turistas* got scared away by Argentina's problems.

When Officer Bustamante stopped us, I knew we were in big trouble. Busti watched Horsey leave, then turned to me and Chino. "Let me see those cards."

My card had my name and picture on it. It said I was an Official Volunteer Tourist Assistant, and it had a red-and-blue seal like the Department of Tourism puts on official tourist business licenses. Chino's card was just like mine.

"Where did you get these?"

Chino suddenly got interested in a potato chip on the pavement and was cracking the edges off with his toe. He let me answer. "We made them."

Bustamante took in a deep breath. "Made them?"

The way he said it, I didn't think he believed me.

"It was my idea, and Chino drew them."

Bustamante's face turned so red it was the color of Chino's magenta crayon.

"That's forgery!"

Chino stopped reshaping the potato chip. "*Cálmate*, Busti. We didn't hurt anybody. You knew what we were doing and never stopped us."

It was true, but he didn't want to hear it. We thought he didn't care what we were doing. As far as the tourists could tell, it looked like we took care of them.

Bustamante got tall and stiff. He waved the cards in our faces.

"I didn't know about these." He puffed a little, and some of the red left his face. "It is one thing to try to make a little money, but this is racketeering. You know what that is?"

I tried to look surprised and shook my head.

Busti looked at the cards again, especially the official seals. "You drew these?"

Chino shrugged.

"He can draw anything," I said. "Give him the right ink and paper, he'll draw a *yanqui* hundred-dollar bill so good you can spend it."

Two army trucks full of soldiers went screaming by us as Busti marched us the two blocks to Papá's warehouse. There sure were a lot of soldiers around—we usually didn't see a lot of them in our part of town—but I was too worried about myself to make anything of it.

Black letters on the sides and front of the white warehouse building spell out *Romanelli Cruise Boats and Water Taxis, Owned and Operated by Ricardo Ro-*

manelli II. Our big summer cruise ship, the *Góndola del Mar,* was moored in front, alongside our company pier. My father's office is on the second floor.

Chino looked at me, I looked at him. From the way he looked, I could tell he felt even worse than I did. It was the end of a very good business.

2

23 MARCH 1976, BUENOS AIRES: ISABEL LEAVES CAPITOL —TANKS ROLL TOWARD BUENOS AIRES. Tanks from outside Buenos Aires were stationed at key points throughout the city this morning. Crews sit quietly with their turrets open. Military leaders call for calm and public support in restoring order to the country. They report that the aim of Operation Aires is to smash subversion in all its forms.

CHINO AND ME ALWAYS CAUGHT HELL FROM THE same guys. The same ones that gave me trouble (called me Rich Boy) gave Chino a hard time because he was poor.

We're a lot alike: the same height, except he's skinny and his teeth are kind of crooked. Course, he's a little darker than me, brown hair, brown eyes, while I'm what Mamá calls ash blond with greenish eyes. We both have birthdays in April: mine the eleventh and his the twenty-first.

Both of our grandfathers came here from Italy a long time ago. Our families are a lot different, though. My father owns a boat company that hires many people. Chino's father cooks at La Barca Restaurant, and he has personal problems. I have a mamá and my little sister, Chichita. Chino only has his father.

We waited at the door for two soldiers to leave Papá's office. I'd always thought of his office as big, but for the first time I saw how small it really was. There was no place to hide. Officer Bustamante stepped into Papá's office.

"Sorry about this, Señor Romanelli, but the boys are in trouble. They were telling the tourists we have a pickpocket problem at the Caminito and then charging them to act as lookouts."

I wanted to argue but kept quiet.

Papá banged his desk and glared at me. "Ahh-Trray?"

I told myself, *Cálmate, cálmate.*

"It is not exactly like that, *Señor.* We did not charge them. We only accepted tips."

"Damn it, Atre!" His voice was loud. "That's beside the point. There are no pickpockets there. Officer Bustamante takes care of that."

"The *turistas* don't know. They thank us."

"No wonder! You scare them!"

"The downtown guides and tourist books all say La Boca is dangerous. They warn people to be careful. We make them feel safe."

Both Papá and Bustamante knew what I said was true because the shop owners complained about the tourist guides all the time.

Bustamante put my ID card on the desk. "Atre says this was his idea and Chino did the drawing."

My father picked it up, turned it over, and handed it back.

"Chino drew that?"

I nodded.

"He can get in a lot of trouble."

Bustamante spoke up. "Not this time, Señor Romanelli. I'm certain fathers know how to handle such problems. If you will excuse me, I have to take Chino to see his father."

"Thanks, Berto. It won't happen again."

Bustamante answered, "No problem, Ricky," and saluted off the bill of his cap.

I hated to see him go. I'd a lot rather have taken whatever Bustamante had to offer than face my father. Papá didn't know about my Caminito money.

My father always said whatever money any of us made was part of the family money. So, whatever me and my sister earned we turned over to him. He gave us what he thought we needed. Of course, if we didn't earn any money, he still gave us what he thought we needed.

My problem was I didn't like asking him for money, so I never told him about the *turista* tips. He only knew about what I earned working around the boats and warehouse.

"I am disappointed in you, Atre."

It would have been better if he was mad. He got mad lots of times. I knew how to handle that 'cause I could always make him laugh. But this was different.

I didn't say anything.

Finally, he said, "Your mother always taps her elbow and calls me stingy. She says I should realize you need

more money. . . . I don't believe her . . . but"—he
paused for a second—"Maybe she is right. . . . so, as
far as today is concerned, I am letting it drop."

I could hardly believe I'd heard him right, but one
look at his face and I knew more was coming.

"You want to be in the tourist business? I will put
you in the tourist business. Next summer you work the
Góndola del Mar as a boat boy, for minimum pay . . .
and it will be family income."

My stomach hurt. If that job sounds like a good
deal, it is only because you don't know about being a
boat boy, fifteen hours a day, mostly cleaning muck
and gunk from engine room bilge bottoms and the
galleys. It's hot and you never get through. You help
take passengers ashore in Mar del Plata. You've got
to be scrubbed clean and smile like you got ten extra
teeth.

You lift old people in and out of the boats, and if
one of them falls down it's your fault. The passengers
treat you like you're a baggage machine. If you get a
tip for carrying a bag ashore, it might be a few pesos at
most. Now, I'd probably have to give those up, too.

He wasn't finished. "It is possible you will earn tips
for carrying luggage ashore. Honestly earned tips are
your money. But, they will be honest. . . . Now, I will
talk to Señor Echavarria and make the same proposal
for Chino."

I checked my sneakers. They needed cleaning. I
knew he wasn't through talking to me.

"Atre, you are too reckless. It is one thing to be

bold and another to take stupid chances. I like your
courage, but you could get in serious trouble for what
you were doing. Lucky for us that Berto Bustamante is
our friend."

He stood up and put a hand on my shoulder. "Have
you seen the truckloads of soldiers? The army is going
to take over the government sooner than people
think." His hand began to grip my shoulder real hard.
I don't think he realized it. "The Generals will not
think *muchachos* hustling tourists is clever. Generals
have no sense of humor."

I looked just below his eyes and nodded so he would
know I listened and understood. I always knew he
liked me being a little reckless. After all, he was the one
who named me Atre. It is a little word he made up for
me, it stands for the word *atreverse,* "to dare."

It was nine more months until summer vacation. I'd
have less money than a shantytown boy during my last
year of *secundaria.* The teenagers I went to school
with already hassled me for living in La Boca. They
had plenty of money, but I had always had enough to
hold my own, until now.

Later that evening I heard what I expected: Señor
Echavarria had agreed to make Chino a boat boy, too.

3

22 APRIL 1976, BUENOS AIRES: The Military Government declares Argentina to be in a "state of war" with guerrilla forces throughout the country. Military spokesmen say they must stop the flow of enemy propaganda and have imposed temporary press censorship. The order takes effect immediately and will remain only as long as absolutely necessary.

THE NEXT DAY, TUESDAY, MARCH 23, 1976, IS A DAY everyone in Argentina remembers. We can tell you exactly what we were doing that morning.

I was eating breakfast, trying to listen to the radio and looking at the *Buenos Aires Herald*. I remember seeing the new movie ad for *Earthquake* and another for *The Towering Inferno*.

Actually, I wasn't reading so much as holding the paper so it looked like I was reading. It gave me a place to put my face while Mamá and Papá argued. It was noisy.

"If you weren't such a miser he wouldn't get into mischief!" Mamá yelled.

"I am not!" he shouted. "And it wasn't mischief. He's a *ladrón!*"

Mamá's face got almost blue. "Ricardo is not a thief! He is money mad . . . *like his father!*"

"Read the newspaper, woman! I'm not thinking about money. I'm thinking about him. This is no time for juvenile pranks."

They were arguing so loud I almost missed it when the music stopped and a voice came on. "All schools, banks, and government offices are closed. All citizens are to stay in their own neighborhoods today."

The voice explained that the army tanks were in the streets for our protection. The army, navy, and air force were taking over the government. We call them the Generals.

I remember thinking how smart my father was. He had said the army would take over pretty soon.

The morning of the coup, while we ate breakfast, there was still an outside chance Papá'd change his mind and not force me to be a boat boy. I wanted Mamá to keep arguing; maybe she'd get him to take it easy on me. She didn't want me gone all summer. I hoped she could talk him into letting me off with one month on the *Góndola del Mar* and maybe get him to loosen up a little with the money he gave me.

Mamá never missed a chance to trash Papá for being stingy. She hated living in La Boca, called it a slum. She said we had enough money to live in a good part of town, except Papá was too *codo*.

Three years before she got so mad she took a job at the *Buenos Aires Herald* translating newspaper stories from Spanish into English. She said she would keep all her own money and buy a better house herself if she had to. My father laughed at her. But he never got any of her money.

The radio announcement ended any chance of Papá changing his mind.

I didn't care who ran the government. A few years later I realized how dumb that was. Something very big had happened, and I didn't have a clue what it meant. At the time, my only thought was seeing the tanks.

Mamá must've read my thoughts, because the first thing she said was "Ricardo, do not go too far from home today. Hear?"

"*Vale,* Mamá." I figured if I got home before dark it wouldn't be too far.

I whispered to my sister, Chichita, "Want to go to the Plaza? See the army tanks?"

"*Sí,* I like the cute tank soldiers in their little red caps."

Mamá snapped at her. "Graciela, you stay away from soldiers. I catch you around an army tank and I will red-cap you!"

Chichita was twelve then, more than a year younger than me, but she looked older, and all she ever talked about was boys.

Nobody called Chichita "Graciela" except Mamá. She was also the only one who called me Ricardo.

When Mamá finished telling me and Chichita what to do, she turned to Papá and said, "It's about time the army stepped in. Things will get better now."

Papá shrugged. I had always thought he liked the army. Lots of times soldiers or sailors came to his office to sell him tickets or something. They told jokes, and he laughed. In fact, that was what he was doing the day before when Officer Bustamante took us to his office.

The music came back on. Both Mamá and Papá left for work after Mamá ordered me and Chichita to clean the house. We worked fast and finished in a hurry.

Now all I had to do was think of a way to make money and not get into trouble.

Chino was waiting for me in front of La Barca Restaurant wearing a sorry look. He tried to smile. I felt like the last tree in Dog Town.

La Barca Restaurant is a block away from the Caminito, but neither one of us wanted to get close to that place. We decided to go down by the Plaza de Mayo.

The Plaza generally had a lot of people going through it. Not that day. It wasn't completely empty, but it had a lot less people than it usually did. Everybody walked fast, like they were in a hurry to get someplace. They didn't act scared or anything, they just kept moving.

Four khaki-colored tanks were parked on each corner of the Plaza. The turrets were open, and the tank commanders sat with their heads sticking up, all of them sergeants. An officer and a soldier holding a walkie-talkie stood beside each tank. No one stopped to look at the tanks or talk to the soldiers.

"Keep moving," Chino said. "We don't want trouble."

"What trouble? The Generals are in charge now. Everything will be better."

I started toward the nearest tank to get a good look. Each one had a big cannon sticking out from the turret and a short machine gun barrel sticking out farther down. The little windows were open so the men inside could see out.

"*Hola,*" I called to the tank commander. He gave a nod and a sort of smile. The sergeant was friendly, but the officer standing next to the tank looked up at him. The gold bars showed the officer was a lieutenant. The sergeant stopped smiling and turned his face away.

"*Cómo le va?*" I asked the lieutenant.

"You live around here?" His voice was grumpy.

"*Sí.* We live near the Obelisco."

I must have made Chino nervous, because he was looking for something on the ground to play with.

The lieutenant's face said he didn't like me. He told us to go home. When we got far enough away so the officer wouldn't hear, Chino asked, "Why'd you tell him we live here?"

"If I said we lived in La Boca, he would've made us go in that direction. Look over your shoulder and you'll see he's still watching us."

Chino took a quick look. "He is."

"Keep going this way. He'll stop looking."

"What if he sees us again? He'll ask for our identification and know we don't live here. I don't want trouble with the army."

"You worry too much, Chino. If we run into him again, I'll think of something."

We moved out of the lieutenant's sight, but there was no way we were going to get away from the army. Every intersection had soldiers, and most had a tank parked in the middle.

Nobody on the streets was relaxed, no window shoppers, but they didn't look unhappy either. A few people waved at the soldiers.

The newsstands were open. Big black newspaper headlines said it was good having the Generals take charge.

We decided to go back home, made a loop around the Plaza de Mayo, and headed toward La Boca.

"Have you thought of a way we can make hard money?"

I shook my head. I saw myself cleaning our water taxis and working in the warehouse after school and weekends for the next fifty years. My guess was Chino's father would put him to work in La Barca kitchen.

"I think I am going to have a year at hard labor. What about you?"

"Me, too," Chino answered. "Kitchen slop and washing dishes. Well, at least we'll work on the cruise boat next summer. That doesn't sound too bad."

"Wait, just you wait. You'll see."

I didn't say so, but if he thought kitchen slop smelled bad wait till he'd been in a ship's bilge. Of course, it wasn't exactly the same for him. He kept the money he made.

"Sorry I got you in trouble."

He looked surprised. "Sorry? What for?"

We said good-bye and went home.

We never talked about it again.

I got home before anyone else, flopped on the couch, and picked up yesterday's *Herald* to practice my English. Mamá always brings a copy home.

It said forty-three people were murdered during the past week, by either left-wing terrorists or right-wing death squads. Four terrorists went in a hospital and machine-gunned a patient. Then it reported that the new million-peso note was going to be worth $170 U.S.

That was baloney. A million pesos wouldn't come close to $170; maybe 140 *yanqui* dollars, at most. I knew that much.

I put the paper down. No wonder everybody felt good about the coup. Argentina was a total mess. Things could only get better.

4

---

15 June 1976, Buenos Aires: *Editorial.* "Has terrorism become an integral part of Argentina?" The chief of federal police was murdered last night, in his home, in his bed. The body of Catholic University Dean, Maria del Carmen Maggi, was found in Mar del Plata. The past three months have seen more than forty civic-official or business-leader assassinations. Montonero guerrillas claim responsibility for killing thirty people in the police headquarters bombing in Pilar.

THE NEXT DAY I HEARD HORSEY ZOLEZZI'S FATHER ran off with a girlfriend. No one ever saw him again.

Just about everybody in La Boca went to church, so the next Sunday I expected a lot of people would hang around afterward and talk about the coup and Señor Zolezzi.

My family always went to church together. Mamá had started keeping Chichita close to her to try to stop her from flirting. But that didn't stop my sister. Her bright eyes, smiles, and swishing skirt said more than words.

People stood around as usual. The little kids climbed on the iron-bar fence that enclosed the front courtyard; men gathered by Admiral Beltrano's big stone tomb, and women bunched up by the front steps. Nobody talked about Señor Zolezzi or the coup. In fact, they only talked about who was sick, who was getting married, who was having a baby. They talked about work, about business, about prices. They talked about the weather, how the climate was changing . . . anything but Señor Zolezzi or the Generals.

When we came out of church, I started to ask my father something and he nudged me to stop. His eyes flicked over toward a green Ford Falcon parked at the curb. Two men in dark suits, *trajes,* got out of the car and leaned against it. Everybody started saying good-bye and left.

We were walking along, close to home, when I asked Papá, "Why didn't anybody say anything about Señor Zolezzi?"

He slowed down, and Mamá and Chichita got farther away from us. "Señor Zolezzi was taken. He didn't run off with a girlfriend. You must promise not to say anything about it to anyone."

"I promise, but why would anyone want Señor Zolezzi?"

"It has something to do with the union. Some of them say they are socialists. Who knows what they do?"

The only thing they did that I knew about was carry picket signs. Still, Señor Zolezzi and Papá were friends. Members of UTP worked for Papá at the warehouse.

"What does *taken* mean? Was he arrested?"

Papá stopped walking, and his face got stern. "Señora Zolezzi said two men, like those outside the church today, broke into their house and took him away."

"To jail?"

"I don't know."

"Are you going to do something?"

The stern look got angry; he was squinting and his eyes got dark. "Do what? I called the police. They don't know anything. Why should I do something?"

"Because you call him your friend. I thought you would do something."

Papá's face got red. "I don't know everything Zolezzi does. Let the union take care of him." He started walking again.

I was quiet for a few steps before asking, "She said men in suits took him?"

"Señora Zolezzi said they took him away in a green Ford Falcon, the kind Army Intelligence drives." He stopped again and grabbed me by both shoulders. "Whatever Zolezzi did is none of your business, so you listen! I gave *my word* to Señora Zolezzi that we would not tell anyone what she told me. Chichita does not know anything about it, and you must not tell her, or anyone. I am telling you this to remind you *to stay out of trouble. No more tourist tricks, nothing. Understand?* And keep your mouth shut."

"*Sí*, Papá. I understand. I promise. I won't tell anyone."

The next morning I was in Gino's drinking *maté* with Chino, and since no one else was there, I told him. "Papa is sure the Generals took Señor Zolezzi.

He thinks talk alone can make a person disappear. Zolezzi was working with some *socia–*" Chino quickly tapped his finger to his mouth, signaling me to shut up.

A *traje* was behind me zipping his pants. The suit had been in the bathroom, and there was no telling what he'd heard. He left just as Busti came by. They both stopped for a second, the suit said something, and then went on his way. I was really scared. Chino started talking about something else. I didn't hear him.

"You think he heard me?"

"I don't know. He didn't act like it. Who knows? Does it matter?"

I swore to myself I would never talk about it ever again.

A few days later Officer Bustamante told people he heard Señor Zolezzi had been arrested but only for a few hours and that then Señor Zolezzi had run off with his girlfriend. Busti said that his information came from higher-ups.

Horsey said it wasn't true, but almost everybody else believed Busti. Nobody ever again heard from Señor Zolezzi, so nobody ever knew for sure.

Things started changing after that. Not all at once but gradually. I saw La Boca people get quiet around strangers. When one came in a store we all stopped talking. That wasn't like us. We had always gotten along with strangers. And everybody stayed away from green Ford Falcons.

The rest of 1976 was so-so. Chino and I turned fourteen in April. My father gave him part-time work at the warehouse. I had lots of time in the evenings for schoolwork.

In October Chino got interested in Japanese painting. As far as I could tell, it was like a lot of other art things he enjoyed.

One holiday Saturday, when we didn't have anything else to do, we went to the Museum of Modern Art. It's in an old factory building not too far from La Boca. Chino was good at art and always liked going to the museum, but this time was different. This time they were showing Japanese art. He saw something in those ink drawings that he really liked.

"Look at this print, Atre!" He pointed to one with a stubby Japanese guy on a little wooden bridge over a skinny river with blue mountains in the background. "See how delicate this is? Look at the colors, soft and yet bright. Magnificent! These are wood-block prints. The artist carves a separate block for each color and then stamps them on ink pads and makes a print on rice paper. Do you like them?"

"I guess so."

"Listen, if I learn how to make these, we can make many copies of anything we want. That has to be worth something."

When we got outside he took a book out from under his shirt titled *Hiroshige Block Prints*.

"Where did you get the book?"

"In the book room."

"What book room?"

"A little room in the back."

I had never seen a little room in the museum, and we went there a lot. I thought about it. "The director's office?"

He nodded. I shook my head. I didn't like him stealing the book. If he got caught, we would both be in trouble. Of course, Chino didn't have much money for things like books. We didn't talk about it anymore.

Chico copied the block prints all year long. He had soft wood and little chisels and carved his own. They were very good.

If it wasn't for me and Chino's Bank of Boston dollar account, I would have been completely broke before December, when summer vacation starts. Lucky for us, some banks offered special accounts for hard money. We didn't lose anything we'd saved. But after the coup we didn't make any more either. And that had been way back in March.

The only new hard money I got during that whole time was from Abuela Romanelli, my grandmother. In April she gave me fourteen *yanqui* dollars. She always gave me and Chichita a dollar for each year on our birthdays. Abuela always said she wished they were hundred-dollar bills instead of one-dollar bills.

Chino and I made a few pesos playing poker. Friday was payday in La Boca. Most of the guys stopped at the Barber Shop Café after work. That's where we gambled.

Working with tourists helped me learn to win at poker. It's all a matter of knowing how to size people up. Like when Horsey hadn't won a pot in an hour and half and his money was nearly gone, that was the time to encourage him. When it was my turn to deal, I always dealt stud poker (one card face down and four cards face up).

I'd say, "Look! Horsey has a jack and a seven, working on a straight." The chances of him getting an eight, nine, and ten to make the straight were almost hopeless, but Horsey was always ready to believe it.

Next card, say he got a deuce, messing up the straight. I'd say, "Watch out for Horsey, one more jack to go with the one he has in the hole and it's three of a kind."

When he heard that his face lit up like a headlight. It didn't matter what his hole card was. He must have felt lucky. The other three jacks could be showing on the table and he'd never see them. He never dropped out and almost never won a hand. He always lost more money than he won. But the hands he won were enough to bring him back.

Some guys are lousy gamblers. You learn to spot the losers and how to talk to them. They are the easiest to push into bigger bets. Knowing how to jab them at the right time with the right word is the way to build big money pots.

Card games are boring, though. And even if I did make money, it was all pesos.

Losing the Caminito business wasn't just losing money either. Mamá was on me all the time. "What is this grade? Eighty-five percent? You accept eighty-five percent? No, no, Ricardo, not eighty-five. . . . Ninety percent. Remember, ninety percent."

School was harder that year than the year before. It was a hard school, the Roosevelt High School, in the Belgrano district, where the embassies are. Lots of *yanquis* went there. Two years before Mamá had put me there, the same private school she'd gone to.

I was definitely from the wrong part of town to go to Roosevelt. It was a long bus and subway ride every day, and I took some insults from a few stuck-ups. Roosevelt was a good school with good teachers. They taught a half day in English and a half day in Spanish. The only problem was you had to have spending money at Roosevelt.

Now that I didn't talk with *turistas,* I didn't get to practice English as much. The way I handled English was good enough, but not as good as the *yanqui* kids. I started reading the *Herald* every day to keep up.

On May 5, 1976, the *Herald* had a tiny story right in the middle of an article on ships docking, like a typesetting mistake. The tiny story said: Harold Conti, a novelist, had been kidnapped by the government, taken from his home, and his whereabouts were unknown. I thought it was a mistake. Kidnapping was against the law.

Argentina was a mess: Somebody tried to bomb President General Videla, again. A paratroop commander in Córdoba burned a bunch of library books. Both my parents were against it, but the commander said they were anti-Argentina books. He said they were against our way of life.

In July, the general's censor came to La Boca School and made the principal get rid of some of the books in the library. One book was called *Cinco Dedos*. It taught little kids how to count on their fingers. The censor took it because he said a closed fist was a Communist signal.

By December the *inflación* had gotten much better. It was down to less than half what it had been in 1975. The *Herald* said the government was doing a good job. Better *inflación* didn't do Chino and me much good, though, not like the old days when we worked the Caminito. We didn't have enough to buy American jeans or concert tickets. By the time school was out in December, we barely had enough money left to go to the movies or buy pizza.

Papá always said, "Smart businessmen know how to make money anytime." And my father was a smart businessman.

Our water taxis always made money. Our vacation cruiser, the *Góndola del Mar,* was always full of people going to Mar del Plata and back. We took them for less money than the newer and larger cruise ships. My father always knew, up to the minute, what things cost and what to charge.

I understood him. A smart businessman should know how to make money. My problem was, and Chino's problem was, we were out of business and it was time to start work on the *Góndola del Mar*.

5

9 SEPTEMBER 1976, BUENOS AIRES: *Editorial.* "It's Time To Talk Frankly." The war is still on. Political murders sweep the country and hooded men pull people from their homes. Terrorists enter hospitals and machine gun patients.

EVERY SEVEN DAYS, AUGUST TO APRIL, SPRING TO fall, the *Góndola del Mar* carried 250 fun-loving passengers from Buenos Aires to Mar del Plata and back, a thousand kilometers round trip. The cruise ship kept them from telephones, television, and newspapers. The everyday ugliness they saw, worried, and kept silent about was left behind.

The crew called them *lobos marinos* because they would lie about like beached sea lions, filling the deck chairs, working on summer tans. They bragged about their boring jobs until a gong called them to eat. The food was excellent: marbled beef, big red lobsters, rich creamy sauces, sugary desserts. They ate like famine was about to strike.

At night they crowded into the small gambling salon to play the slot machines. When they got to Mar del Plata they rushed to the giant government-owned casino to gamble some more.

We always left Buenos Aires at noon sharp Sundays

and returned at 11:00 A.M. Saturdays. Each guest left with something to talk about for another year. Business was good that season. The passengers loved our ship.

The first trip for Chino and me started December fifth. Once we left the Río de la Plata and changed our heading to south-southwest, the Atlantic air turned salty fresh and the bright summer sun started baking oily bodies as they came on deck. The skies were always the color of blue ice, and cool breezes came up from Antarctica driving away the sticky city sweat.

Of course I didn't get to enjoy much of that. Me and Chino spent most days sliding over bilge bottom slime or feeding buckets of sour garbage to fish. We hopped to the orders of our boss, the ship's chief bo'-sun's mate. "Boats" is what everybody called him.

The ship was sparkling white with three upper decks, 1,145 tons, 92 meters long, and a 16-meter beam. The *Góndola del Mar* was not as big as most cruise ships but bigger than a ferryboat. Her crew came from around the world: Argentine officers, Asian cooks, Philippine stewards, and deckhands from everywhere.

Except for officers and stewards, crew orders were to keep away from passengers. For me and Chino that meant all the time except when picking up trash or if early risers came out to watch the sunrise while we sanded the teak decks. It was slow, hard work.

Boat boys only talked to passengers as they went ashore and returned to the ship on the *barcazas*. But even though we didn't talk to them, they knew who we were.

Chino and I were bow hooks on the ship's two *barcazas*. A bow hook stands on the front with a foot planted on each side of the bow and holds the boat to the gangway so the passengers can load and unload.

We wore white pants and blue T-shirts on the *barcazas*. Otherwise we wore only shorts on deck. In five days we were tan. After two weeks we were both brown as saddle leather.

In December and January the *Góndola del Mar* carried a lot of *yanqui* and *jonnie turistas* who came to Argentina to get warm. We loaded the first *yanquis* on our second trip.

Chino and I were sanding the sundeck early the second morning when I heard a lady talking.

"Look dear! Natives. I didn't realize there were primitives living in Argentina." She wore bug-eye mirror glasses under a big straw hat tied down with a purple scarf. Her head looked like it belonged on an insect.

Chino knew she was talking about us, but he didn't know English. "What did she say?"

"She thinks we're natives."

"*Indios?*"

"Maybe Indian. Maybe she's lost, thinks we're in the South Seas."

He laughed. "Probably thinks we swim and fish all the time, like on TV."

I pushed the sanding stone a couple times, thinking about South Sea movies.

"Chino, what do the South Sea *hombres* do in the movies?"

He thought a bit. "Paddle out to ships and dive for money."

"Well, if they want natives, why not us?"

"Doing what?"

"Diving for *yanqui* and *jonnie* coins. It is hard money."

Chino smiled, then he scowled. "How far do we dive?"

"From the *barcaza*. Maybe the main deck."

He shuddered. "I don't mind swimming, but I never like high places. You ever dream you were falling and never stopped? Do you know how that feels?"

I knew, but I didn't tell him. Instead I said, "The main deck is no higher than the five-meter crossbar on La Boca Bridge. You did that." It wasn't really fair because I knew he hated high places. The bridge dive was something we all did to prove we weren't scared. Always on a dare.

He thought about it before making up his mind. High places made his stomach queasy. I was sure he was figuring out how much money we could make. Chino liked money more than he hated high places.

"Just remember not to look down, keep your body

straight, and split the water with your fingertips. You slip in fast and easy."

"Huh! Easy for you to say. You're on a school swim team. You even dive. I don't go to a fancy school with swimming pools and diving platforms. What if I hit wrong? It can hurt bad, *hombre*."

"You can do it. Come on, we could make lots of money. You think Boats will let us work as bow hooks in our swim trunks if we tell him why?"

"*Cómo no?* He knows your father owns the ship."

A couple seconds later he held his palm up, and we slapped. "*Suerte.*"

The lady watched us and touched the man's arm. "Is that a native custom?"

The man must have been her husband because his outfit went with her head: baggy purple shorts and a shirt covered with stars printed in neon colors. "It's a hand greeting between young men, my sweet. Even native boys like these."

"That one looks a bit European. See his hair and eyes?"

"I'm certain these are natives: square features, perfect skin color. No doubt the lighter one's father was a sailor and his mother a native girl."

"What'd they say?" Chino asked.

"Nothing. They talk like schoolteachers."

Chino nodded, and we kept on sanding.

Later that day I asked Boats if me and Chino could put on a show for the passengers in Mar del Plata. I told him our plan and he said OK.

It worked. I gave Boats a couple of *yanqui* quarters
to get it going. When the *barcazas* came alongside,
Boats yelled, "Hey, Fiji! Get this!" and he threw one
quarter in the water next to Chino's boat. Then he
yelled, "Tonga! For you!" and he threw the other one
next to mine.

The two of us hit the water, Plunk! Plunk! The silver
coins spun around underwater and were easy to see. As
soon as we cleared the surface, each of us held up a
quarter and shouted, *"Yanqui! Yanqui!"*

The water was terrific, clear, sky colored, nothing
like the Río Riachuelo in La Boca. The salt tasted
good, and the ocean water fizzed on my skin. We were
no more back in the boats than someone else yelled
and threw two more coins. Then people tried hurrying
us and confusing us by throwing two coins at each of
us. We made six *yanqui* dollars on the first shore boat
trip.

The next day every passenger knew us as Tonga and
Fiji, even the teenage girls. Before then we saw the
girls but they hadn't noticed us. Some were good
looking. In fact most were very good looking, with
blond hair and straight white teeth, or they would be
when the braces came off.

The instant the captain saw us surrounded by girls
he set Boats on us. "Captain says passengers are out
of bounds, mates, especially good-looking teenage girl
passengers and especially to you two. Orders! Got it?"

We both nodded, but Chino pleaded, "But, Boats!
There are so many. . . . I mean, well, uh, what I mean

is, it is only natural to like girls. And, in case the captain didn't notice, they came to us. Like flowers to the bees."

Boats shook his head, mumbling, "Jeez! Flowers to the bees?" And in a somewhat louder voice, "Mates! You two stay away from girl passengers."

"*Mierda!*" Chino mumbled.

We anchored three days a week in Mar del Plata: Tuesdays, Wednesdays, and Thursdays. The diving money was pretty good but still not like what we'd made every summer week at the Caminito.

The cruise between Buenos Aires and Mar del Plata was always misery. The engine room heat reminded me of a steam kettle. Work was nothing but hot slop and slime. But it had a good side we didn't think about. We were away from the city and the Dirty War. That is what some people had started calling it. A war where you don't know whose side you are on. A war that makes you afraid to talk because talk alone can make you disappear.

Our Tonga-Fiji act made anchoring in Mar del Plata something to look forward to. It didn't last long, but it was fun.

When the ship made its last turn to the anchorage, where the ocean's deep blue color got lighter, it headed straight for the Mar del Plata harbor. Boat crews would go to the back of the ship and wait on the fantail for the anchor to drop. We helped swing the *barcazas* out over the water and lower them. It was always a relief to feel the ship heel over a little as it made the last turn.

On our third trip we saw something at the last turn we didn't understand. A big helicopter came at us from the Mar del Plata navy barracks. It looked like a giant banana with pinwheels at each end. It went right overhead so low I saw the pilot's face. He looked bored and sad at the same time, the way I felt in the engine room.

I turned around looking forward until Chino touched me a few minutes later.

"Who is jumping out of the banana?"

It was almost out of sight, but something went out of the helicopter into the ocean.

"Maybe they are Navy *Focas?*"

"Are you *loco?* Navy Seals don't dive that high. Nobody gets paid enough to dive that high."

Then another dropped out of the helicopter and another. I couldn't tell if they were men or not, so I asked Boats.

Boats shook his head. "Too high for *Focas;* they jump from ten meters. That bird is two hundred and fifty meters up. Somebody left the doors open." He turned quickly and went forward like he didn't want to talk anymore.

Chino watched, spellbound. "They've got to be *loco.*"

We saw more and more bananas flying in and out of the Mar del Plata Barracks that summer, more on every trip, but we didn't see any more Navy *Focas*. Chino said maybe they stopped practicing.

About a week before Christmas we got lucky. A *jonnie* passenger was betting with a *yanqui turista,* and he kept daring us to take bigger chances. We learned how to make a lot of hard money from him.

The *jonnie* wanted us to dive from the boat deck. The *Góndola del Mar* had three layers above the main deck: boat, promenade, and sun decks. Each higher level set in a little from the one underneath. The higher the deck the farther out you had to go to miss hitting a railing as you went by. It was dangerous.

The *jonnie* held up two coins, two *jonnie* pounds. "How about it?"

I looked at Chino.

"*Vale*, Atre." He crossed himself. "I'll try it once." The expression on his face said the only reason he was diving was to keep from looking chicken.

We took off from the second deck, springing our legs as hard as possible. Chino barely cleared the main deck rail. Each of us got a coin about two meters underwater. For me the dive was almost better than the money. I loved it.

Chino wasn't smiling. "*Nunca más!*" he said, and he meant it. Getting that close to the rail would make anybody think about how much they'd risk for two dollars.

I wasn't through diving myself, though, not yet.
There's something about falling through the air
and the feel of cool water when it touches your fingers,
then your whole body, you bend a little to get back
up, and the taste of fresh air when you break the surface. Boy! That's fun.

Boats gave me the OK to talk to the *jonnie*. If I was
right the guy was a pure gambler. He'd bet on anything.

"I bet I can get three *jonnies* at once from the top
of the wheelhouse on the sundeck. If I get them you
owe me three more, six pounds altogether. If I do not,
I give you back your three pounds."

A smile bent across his mouth, and his eyes flickered.
He held out a hand, and we shook. He turned to the
man beside him and bet a hundred *yanqui* dollars on
me.

I leaped way out to miss the railings. A quick
whoosh of air fluttered on my body as I went by the
main deck. I barely cleared it by a finger width.

Once in the water I had all the time in the world to
get those coins. That gambler roared when he saw
them in my hand. He didn't even look at the other
man, just put out his hand and collected his hundred
dollars.

Chino helped me climb aboard his *barcaza* to catch
my breath. A woman passenger took our picture with
a Polaroid and gave us each a copy. Maybe we did look
a little bit native.

That was our last trip before Christmas 1976.

.   .   .

Christmas came on Saturday that year, and I got to go
home for the day. When I got there, Uncle Fredo's air
force car was parked in front. The whole family was
inside, including Abuela, my aunt Nina, Uncle Fredo,
and my baby cousin.

As soon as she saw me, Mamá started crying and got
mad at Papá, again.

"You do not even pay him, you stingy—" She held
her elbow up and was about to pat it when Papá
reached in his shirt pocket and handed her a small
brown velvet bag. She pulled the drawstrings open and
took out a gold key. "What is this?"

"That, Señora Spend-It-All, is the key to your fancy
sixteen-room house in Mar del Plata, in the best part
of town."

Mamá was speechless. Her arm dropped.

I couldn't believe it. Papá spent money on a house?
It must have cost over a hundred thousand *yanqui* dollars. Were we really going to move? Live with rich people? Leave La Boca?

Chichita squealed, "When? When?"

"*Cálmate, mija.* It will take time. But it will be our
new home soon as the improvements are finished."

The house got noisy as a football game. My uncles
followed Papá to the kitchen for brandy. The women
were all fluttery. The *niños* were happy for about one
second and then started asking to open presents.

Mamá cried. She cried so much I couldn't tell for

sure what she said. It sounded like "(Sob) . . . A Mar del Plata home (sob, sob) is more than I dreeeeamed . . . (sob, sob)."

When I heard Mamá say Mar del Plata, I thought about what it meant to go there, who I'd leave behind. "Papá, how long before we move?"

"At least six months, maybe longer. It takes time to put in an up-to-date kitchen, refinish all the rooms, put in new bathroom fixtures, and landscape the yard. The work will not begin until I receive the paper that says we own the house. The agent transferred title to our name yesterday. We will get the deed in a few days."

6

13 SEPTEMBER 1976, BUENOS AIRES: The *Osaka Maru,* a Japanese freighter carrying a cargo of automobiles, will dock at pier seventy-six this morning. Yesterday, city police gunned down an unnamed man as he painted antigovernment slogans on a west side warehouse. According to observers, the police issued no warnings before opening fire. The next shipment of Japanese cars is not expected for several months.

THE *GÓNDOLA DEL MAR* MUSICIANS PLAYED FROM nine at night until three o'clock the next morning for the 1977 New Year's celebration. The passengers wore party hats and carried noisemakers in one hand and drinks in the other. They hopped around the dance floor like fleas on wet sand. The galley crew worked overtime keeping the buffet tables full.

It was a Friday night, and we were looking in on somebody else's party. It was awful.

The ship was in Buenos Aires Harbor all New Year's Day, so we got to go home for the second time in eight days. Three days later we were back in Mar del Plata.

Chino went with me to see our new house. A Mercedes-Benz was parked in front with a man sitting behind the wheel. I thought it was just another fancy car in a fancy neighborhood.

I pushed the front gate open, and we started to go in the yard when he yelled at us, "Who are you and what you doing here?"

"I'm Ricardo Romanelli, same as my father. We own this house."

The man got friendly. "A general?"

"No. Why?"

"Generals, admirals, or brigadiers buy houses in this neighborhood. Is he an admiral?"

"No. We own water taxis and a cruise ship."

"Oh? A businessman? Well, that's an interesting change. Sorry you can't get inside today. The house-keeper has the keys, and she's not here."

"*Vale,* we'll look at the outside."

Most of the building was hidden behind the trees and large bushes that surrounded the entire lot. I was really impressed. In front was a round fishpond, as big as a helicopter pad. The house was two stories of gray limestone blocks, sixteen rooms and five bathrooms. An elephant could walk in the front door without touching either side.

"This is really yours?" Chino asked.

I nodded.

"You won't ever come back to La Boca."

"You know I will. Besides, we won't move for a long time. There's a lot to do before we move, and even when we do it's not far to Buenos Aires."

"Too far to walk."

"Planes, buses, and trains go every day. You see the bananas go back and forth all the time."

He didn't say anything.

"An hour plane ride, maybe less."

"How long by bus?"

"Five hours."

"I'll take a bus."

Each time we anchored in Mar del Plata, Chino helped me set up my high dive bet with a passenger. We made a lot of hard money. He only dove from the boat deck that one time.

Later he asked, "Why do they pay us for diving, Atre?"

"For fun, what else? Some people like to gamble, and some pay to see us get hurt."

He shuddered, didn't even want to think about it. Diving from the main deck for money was as much as he could take.

When summer ended we each had over $240 U.S.

My father complained about the deed to our Mar del Plata house still not coming and it was late January. He called the Property Registration Office. They said they were working on it.

Mamá was more patient. "Ricky, you know better

than to expect the government to do anything in a hurry. Do something to make yourself feel good. Go count your money."

The Generals made up some new rules. The censor stopped us from buying Beatles' records, said their words were subversive, gave us bad ideas. The censor was brain warped.

Next thing, in February, the Generals shut down *La Opiñon* newspaper for two days because it printed something about human rights. I guess the Generals didn't like people reading about human rights.

By March 1977, when summer ended, I think everybody knew things were bad in Argentina, and not just money-wise. Seeing a green Falcon stop anywhere close to you was scary.

By this time everybody knew about people being taken out of their houses while their families watched. The police always said they didn't know anything. If someone got arrested, really put under arrest, it was a relief, because getting arrested meant they wouldn't disappear. No telling how many did disappear: teachers, students, priests, union leaders, anybody.

Nobody talked about it, but I could see it in their faces. We all knew of people who disappeared for no reason. Most of the missing were never heard from again, ever. But we acted as if nothing was happening. We still stopped in the street to talk. We still went to

cafés and talked, like always, except nobody talked
about politics anymore. Nobody talked about the
Generals.

The Dirty War was everywhere. Many people were
afraid. The *Herald* said we all deserved answers. I
didn't know who to believe, so I believed what I saw.
On the ship I lived a sailor's life. On land, the Dirty
War went on all around me.

Saturday, March fifth, we left the *Góndola del Mar* to
go back and start *colegio*. I was going to Roosevelt
High School, but Chino had a scholarship to Santa
Maria Colegio, a Catholic high school near La Boca.
He got in free for being a good artist. Chino called
Roosevelt *Rose-ah-belda*. Roosevelt is hard to say in
Spanish.

We knew we wouldn't see much of each other once
school began. We decided to go help each other register.

The next Monday morning we took the downtown
subway out to Roosevelt High School. Chino talked
to a blond girl sitting across from us. I was reading an
editorial in the *Herald* titled "Let's Face Reality." It
said sixty-nine people had disappeared in two days and
nobody would tell where they were. It said Argentina
lived with horrors that were now considered normal.
The guerrilla war was over. The guerrillas were supposed to be the reason the Generals took over the gov-

ernment in the first place. We were as far from peace as ever. The editorial finally asked the Generals to explain just what they were doing.

Mamá said green Falcons parked in front of the *Herald* building every night.

I wore my regular school uniform to go register. All schools in Argentina have uniforms. Roosevelt boys wore green sweaters, white shirts, and gray pants. Chino wore jeans, T-shirt, and sneakers.

Chino looked around the school office while I filled out registration papers. My classmate Howard Klone came in.

"Oh, boy! *Mozo!* Come get these boxes." He was talking to Chino, but Chino didn't know it.

"Say! *Mozo!* Did you hear me? Come get these boxes."

I turned around. "Howie! That's my friend you're talking to. He isn't your handyman. His name's Chino."

When he heard his name, Chino gave Howie a seventeen-tooth grin and held out his hand, palm up, waiting for the slap.

Howard Klone was definitely not a native; he didn't even have dark hair (it was red), and he hadn't learned hand slapping. So, the hand slap never came. Instead, he shook hands with Chino but afterward, the way he examined his hand, you would have thought he was looking for bugs.

"Is your friend from La Boca or from the slaughterhouses on the other side of the river?"

Good thing for Howie that he spoke English or

Chino would have decked him. And wouldn't you know it? While Howie was insulting him in English, Chino was bringing in Howie's book boxes.

Howie held out a thousand pesos for a tip.

Chino was smiling all the time until he saw the tip. He slapped Howie's hand with a loud whack, sending the peso note fluttering. He glared at Howie. *"Pendejo!"*

Howie was actually confused. His eyes opened wide, his jaw dropped, he held his hands up in a pleading sort of way. I don't think he got it. He said, *"Lo siento! Lo siento!"* over and over.

Then Chino and I caught a bus to Santa Maria Colegio so he could register. He was quiet on the bus. Not until we were all the way back across town and walking to his school did he say anything. "You see the *rojo*'s sneakers?"

"Howie's shoes? They were red."

"Sí. I would like to have a pair. They were Nike running shoes from the States. The best."

"You want red shoes?"

"Sí, que bueno! Red Nikes with white trim, bright red and pure white."

"Buy them. You have money."

"You know me better than that. Nike running shoes cost forty *yanqui* dollars."

"How much will you pay?"

"Twenty dollars. That's all I can pay. I still have to buy school uniforms and save spending money for the year. I can't buy forty-dollar shoes."

He stopped on the school steps. "Atre, I hate being poor. You know that? I hate it!"

I had never heard him say that before. Howard Klone had really hurt him. Howie was a jerk, but his insults were mostly accidents. He didn't try to hurt anyone's feelings.

"Howie's not a bad person, Chino. He's dumb."

Chino turned his head and looked at me out of the corners of his eyes. "*Mierda!* With all his money? You know he's not dumb. You can't have money like him and be dumb."

I followed him inside Santa Maria Colegio. Father Gonzaga, the headmaster, was glad to see Chino. He pushed the button on his intercom, called someone's name, and a nun came to his office. She was the art teacher, Sister Alicia. The way she and Father Gonzaga talked about Chino's art was enough to make anybody feel good.

Father took Chino into his office and gave him vouchers to pay for schoolbooks and supplies, but that didn't include the uniform. Chino had to buy his own school clothes. Santa Maria uniforms were blue sweater, gray pants, white shirt with red and blue necktie. Most students wore black shoes, but red would look fine if he would spend the money.

The next morning Chino was so excited he looked like a *turista* on New Year's Eve. He had found a way to get enough money to buy the red Nike running shoes he wanted. It had to be a lot of money, because I always got half.

The words jumped out of his mouth. "I saw Horsey with many *yanqui* dollars last night."

"Where did he get *yanqui* money?"

"He said he earned it at the Caminito, but he probably mugged a *turista*."

"How much was it?"

"I saw *yanqui* twenties when he was showing it, only for a second, but it was five bills. He looked like he was waving a winning poker hand for everybody to see. . . . Think of something. How do we get it?"

"Hold on a minute. His old man is gone. Maybe the Zolezzis need the money."

Chino looked disgusted. "Atre! The union gives them money. They don't think old man Zolezzi went away with a girlfriend. I heard union *hombres* say he disappeared. Now, what about Horsey's money?"

"*Cálmate, cálmate*. You just told me. . . . Give me a second. You said twenties?"

Chino started doing little heel bounces. "*Sí, sí*, I counted two twenties and some others I couldn't see."

"We can't try and get it all at once. He'll get suspicious."

Chino stopped bouncing, rolled his eyeballs way up in his head, and drew down the corners of his mouth.

"Chino, if he has the tiniest hint we know about his money, he'll know we're going to try to get it. Did he show it to you?"

"No. He was showing some others when I went by. I wasn't that close. I don't think he saw me."

"Good. Now, where's the first place he'll go this morning?"

He poked a thumb over his shoulder toward Gino's Barber Shop Café. "There, where he can start spending it."

We took off for the café. It was eight-thirty, and we wanted to be there before Horsey. We ordered *maté* and waited.

Chino knew where to sit. He would be on one side of Horsey with me on the other. That way we could see each other and Horsey couldn't see both of us at the same time. We had done this before. Positioning was part of our approach to the *turistas* when we offered to watch out for pickpockets.

We waited, and I thought about what Chino had said about Señor Zolezzi. "Chino, do you believe what you heard the union men say about Señor Zolezzi?"

"Who knows? I do know they're not short of money. . . . Please figure out how we get it from Horsey."

I tried to think of something. What could we do with Horsey? He was a bully, greedy, and a lousy gambler. Then I got it.

"We'll do a bridge dive."

Chino's face wrinkled up. "I don't know . . ."

"This is the time, *compadre*. If we do it right, we get the whole forty dollars. Did you ever see Horsey on the bridge?"

"He dove off from five meters once on a chicken bet."

"Right, one time on a dare. Now, can you handle it?"

7

14 September 1976, Buenos Aires: *Editorial.* "Hidden Motives?" Nine policemen were killed yesterday when a car bomb exploded outside a downtown precinct. The real motivation for this act may be to reactivate the right-wing death squads. Meanwhile, the majority of the nation's magistrates remain idle, waiting for the government to approve of their moral and professional qualifications before letting them return to the courts.

THE OLD BRIDGE IS THE FIRST THING YOU SEE WHEN you get to La Boca. It looks like it's made of giant Lego blocks, a monster loaf of black bread on stilts. It is easy to climb, which we all did sometimes, and it stretches over the dirtiest river in South America, the Riachuelo.

La Boca is hardly what you'd call a river resort. The wet part of the Riachuelo is more diesel fuel than water, but that's not all. The floating parts are what everybody throws in from Paraguay to Buenos Aires. The river comes down from the north, through La Boca, and out to the Río de la Plata.

It is deep enough to handle the midsize freighters and saltwater fishing boats that come tie up in La Boca to get rid of barnacles. Fresh water and diesel fuel kills the barnacles in a matter of days, and that's a whole lot cheaper than hauling and scraping.

The bridge is tall enough for some ships to pass under, about fifteen meters from the water to the roadbed above. Only a few guys ever dive off, and only on a dare and a bet. Fewer still ever dove from above five meters and never more than ten.

Our plan was to dare Horsey into a high dive bet, get him scared, and switch the dare around. I knew he wouldn't jump.

"How high?" Chino asked.

"From the roadbed."

His gasp was so loud Gino looked up. Then Chino whispered, "The *roadbed*? Atre, that's over *ten meters*!"

"Don't worry, it's straight down, no railing to look out for. Just keep your eyes straight ahead when you climb. A high dive is a high dive, right?"

"Is falling off a ten-story building the same as falling off a one-story building?"

"You want the money?"

Chino was quiet for almost a full minute. I knew he didn't want to do it. "Why do you want to do this?"

"Because it's sure to work with Horsey."

He wouldn't look at me. I guessed he was trying to think of a good reason not to dive.

Before he could say no I added, "Remember, we're talking about *forty U.S. dollars*. We can get the whole *forty* dollars."

Chino's expression went *tilt* for about ten seconds; then the lines around his mouth started to get tight again. I knew he was still thinking of a way to get out of it, so I went on. "I'm telling you, if we do it we'll get it all."

He was still grim. At last he looked up and gave that seventeen-tooth smile of his. "For a pair of Nike running shoes, what's one more nightmare? *Suerte!*"

When Horsey Zolezzi came in the Barber Shop Café, he looked like a tall dog with a big bone.

"Congratulations, Horsey!" I said it real loud, with all the enthusiasm I could put in it.

Horsey's face got stiff. "Uuh," he growled. "I got lucky."

"What branch you going into?" I asked.

"What do you mean, branch? What branch?"

"The military. Today's your birthday, isn't it? The year you get called for military service?"

"No, *estúpido,* it's not my birthday . . . as if you care!"

I shrugged to show him I didn't have a lot of interest. "You're right, Horsey, I don't, but the way you came here all puffed up, I guessed it must be your birthday. I was wrong. Forget it. I wasn't getting you a present anyway. . . .

"Besides, you interrupted. Me and Chino have been talking about which branch we want to get into when we have to do national service. I definitely want the paratroops. They wear great uniforms. I love those green berets and short boots."

Horsey nodded and signaled Gino to bring him a Pepsi. We all liked paratrooper uniforms.

I kept going. "Horsey, you'd never make a para-trooper. It's pretty clear to me what the army's going to do with you. You'll dig latrines for the real soldiers."

The instant he opened his mouth, I knew we had him. "Oh yeah! Oh yeah! Well I'd be twice the para-trooper you would, Romanelli. They're never going to let you be a paratrooper. You'd steal parachutes and sell them for yard umbrellas."

Once Horsey's mad he's a chicken in a car wash, a mass of wet feathers and squawks.

"You're afraid of heights, Zolezzi. You can't be a paratrooper and be afraid of getting off the ground."

Chino added, "Come to think of it, Hector, I don't remember ever seeing you on the bridge."

"Liar! I've been up there lots of times. I was on the bridge. You know I dove off the five-meter bar. I'm no chicken."

I reached over and patted his shoulder. "Horsey, Horsey, *cálmate*. We know you were on the bridge. Everybody does it. That's not what we're talking about. How about diving from the old roadbed? Para-troopers jump that far into a sandbox. Diving into water is a snap."

His complexion turned a shade greener than the *maté* I was drinking.

"Uoh! Uoh!" He sounded like a goose giving a half a honk. Horsey was always a man of a few words.

I pulled my chair up close and leaned over. "I'll bet you ten *jonnies* you're too scared."

"Oho? Oho?"

I leaned my chair back, looking real confident, and turned to Chino. "It wouldn't take me long to make that bet. I'd take it in a snap. Course, I'm not a *smart* gambler like Horsey."

"Ooooh! Ooooh!" This time he said it like somebody just called a guard dog off his chest. "Listen, Rich Boy, I'll bet neither you or the Stick will do it, and I'll bet you twenty *yanqui* dollars."

I put my chair down on four legs and slid back. I heard Chino's chair legs squeal on the floor at the same time. This is what we called the pullback. The hook was going in, so to speak. The object was to set it so he didn't get away.

We both looked at him with the expressions we had practiced. Our faces said we didn't believe him, but we didn't dare say it out loud. We wanted to keep quiet and wait for my answer.

A little silence, then: "You have twenty *yanqui* dollars, Horsey?"

"*Sí!* I have twenty *yanqui* dollars."

I gulped loud so Horsey could hear it and heard Chino do the same. We shifted to our next face, the scared look.

"*Perdón,* Horsey," I said. "I wasn't sure you meant it. I wouldn't risk my life and not have you pay."

"Don't worry. Gino will hold the money. I'll collect as soon as you give up."

Chino spoke up like an actor on cue. "You sure you want to do this, Atre? It must be *fifty meters* to the water. You could get killed!"

Horsey didn't say anything about fifteen meters being called fifty. He didn't know how high it was.

"*Amigo,* I can't back down. I couldn't face anybody if I backed down."

"Yes you can. It's no shame to keep from breaking your neck."

Horsey's head was darting back and forth between us like a kid in a candy store.

"Maybe I did bet too soon. I've never dove *fifty meters* before."

Horsey quickly handed a *yanqui* twenty to Gino, who was watching the whole thing.

Horsey shouted, "A bet is a bet! The dive's a snap. Like jumping in a sandbox."

I reached in my pocket for the *jonnie* ten-pound note, handed it to Gino, and hung my head. I winked at Chino, who was trying hard not to smile. Gino saw us, but Horsey didn't.

The old bridge was a long block away. By the time we got there, a bunch of *jovenes* and little kids were waiting. Everybody knew the bet was on. I swaggered as I walked to the black iron crossbars and turned to face Horsey again. "I'll have a good time spending your *yanqui* twenty."

Chino stood behind the group of watchers. As I put my right foot on the first crossbar, he spoke up in a voice loud enough for everyone to hear: "Glad I'm not diving."

It went just as we'd planned. Horsey swallowed the hook. "You are diving, *pendejo*. Who said any different?"

"What?" I shouted and stopped climbing.

"You both dive off the top of the bridge."

"Now hold on a minute, Hector. I said *I'd* dive from the roadbed, not Chino."

Horsey relaxed and got a big smile. "Going to turn chicken, huh? I thought so. I'll go get my money from Gino."

I gave him my broken-down look. "Go ahead! Take the money."

Chino rushed up to Horsey. "No! No! I'm not afraid."

All the guys cheered. They wanted to see us get killed more than they wanted to see Horsey lose twenty dollars.

"It'll cost you another twenty," I said.

"What for? A bet is a bet."

"You bet *me* twenty dollars against *my jonnie* ten pounds. If Chino dives, you put up twenty for him."

"Oh? Oh? And what does he put up?"

"His body, you idiot! He's betting his life against a stinking twenty *yanqui* dollars. Ask the guys, isn't that fair?"

"Yeah! Yeah!" everybody shouted. At this point they had a great show no matter what happened.

The hook was all the way down in his gut, and he couldn't cough it up. He had to put up the other twenty or be chicken. He handed the second bill to

Gino, who had closed the café and come to watch the show.

We stripped to our shorts, left our clothes by the fireboat, where we could wash off when we got out of the water, and climbed the old bridge, hand over hand, up one metal bar to the next.

Chino asked, "How did you know he would make me dive, too?"

"Simple. Horsey likes money, but he's not a gambler. By the time he realized what he'd done, he knew he'd lose. The only thing left was for him to try and get you to dive. He knows you never liked diving. He was praying one of us would back down."

We got to the roadbed. For the first time I saw it was more than fifteen meters, more like twenty meters above the water, a long, long, long way down. "You scared?" I asked.

"Shut up and count!" He snapped back.

We counted together, "One, two, three," and took off from either side of the bridge.

It was terrific. It felt like a hundred meters. I could have stayed in the air forever.

The smell of diesel fuel got to me just before my fingertips hit the water. I closed my eyes, thinking the Riachuelo would probably dissolve my eyeballs. I remember thinking about Chino, hoping he'd closed his eyes and sorry I hadn't said anything to him.

My body lifted up toward the surface, and I felt something big against my arm, kind of soft, like a huge water balloon. My right hand touched it. It felt like a person's arm.

Oh, my God! I thought. It's Chino!

I grabbed hold of Chino's body and kicked my legs to get to the surface. As my head broke clear, I heard the boys shouting, and then I heard Chino yell, "We made it! We made it!"

If that's Chino over there, I asked myself, who am I holding?

My hand let go, and a man's body floated to the surface.

It didn't look much like a person, swollen so that the yellow shirt was all filled out and stretched tight. It had no pants on, only shorts. It floated like a rubber duck in a bathtub. It wasn't real, not like a person. I pushed at the shoulder to get it over by the bank where we could get it out.

Chino came to help. We slid the body up, and Chino yelled at Gino to go call Bustamante.

The guys on the opposite bank had to get in a rowboat to come over. They came over four or five at a time to look at the body. I told them no. It didn't seem right to stand around looking at it. Besides, it was an awful looking thing. Waiting for the police took forever.

A few minutes later we heard the *wowowow* of the police coming. An ambulance was right behind. Bustamante asked us a couple questions. Gino was back from calling the police by then. He said the same as us. Bustamante said it was a Montonero murder victim. An ambulance took the body away.

We washed off with the fire hose, threw our dirty shorts in the river, and Gino gave us Horsey's forty *yanqui* dollars. We got happy again.

We started toward Avenida Florida so Chino could get his red-and-white Nike running shoes.

"Atre, don't do that again."

"You mean it? No more diving? Never?"

"Well, summers on the ship, main deck only, no more."

"What's wrong with diving?"

I guess he didn't want to talk about it, because he changed the subject. "You saw the spots on that body?"

"What spots? I didn't see spots."

"Small round spots, little holes with white edges. Did you see the long black marks on his legs?"

"Shut up, you're making me sick."

But he didn't stop. "Did you see the feet? They were white, like eggshells, and kind of shriveled, like they were cooked or something."

"For God's sake, stop it."

He didn't say anything more about it. He changed the subject again. "You know, Atre, it's great having money."

I started talking about money, and he started talking

about Nike high-tops. Forty *yanqui* dollars was a real score.

I tried not to think about the man in the yellow shirt, but I could still see him. I still felt his squishy skin. I saw the spots Chino had seen. The man in the Riachuelo was the first thing in the Dirty War that actually touched me.

8

19 SEPTEMBER 1976, BUENOS AIRES: Patricia Ann Erb, nineteen, a United States citizen, was taken from her home today by eight unidentified armed men. Her two brothers and a maid were tied up and left in the home. Miss Erb is the daughter of Pastor John Delbert Erb. Her whereabouts are unknown and there is no further information regarding the men who took her. The kidnapping was reported to police.

NOBODY'S CONFIDENCE EVER GOT SO BIG FROM wearing new shoes. Chino wore his Nikes like a soldier wears a new medal. He cleaned them every morning, kept them bright red and snow white. He thought the Nikes made him look rich. I never thought he looked poor.

Abuela Romanelli gave me fifteen one-dollar bills for my birthday. She always ironed them so they looked new. "If I were rich these would be new one-hundred-dollar bills. Happy birthday."

My parents gave me two new shirts and some new socks. Abuela looked at Papá and tapped her elbow. "Just like your father," she told him.

He ignored her insult and changed the subject. "How is La Vieja Zolezzi?"

Abuela looked down her nose at him. "As if you

care! What have *you* done about Señor Zolezzi disappearing?"

He shrugged and said nothing.

Abuela turned to Mamá, her old, dark eyes flashing anger, and her face said Mamá should answer as well.

"What could we do?" Mamá asked.

"Some friends you are. Thugs take him away and his neighbors do nothing! You like the Fascists?" she said and spat. Abuela always spat when she said *Fascist,* always, like spitting was part of the word, "Fascist-(spit)."

"What is a Fascist-(spit)?" Chichita asked.

Mamá spoke up before Abuela got started spitting Fascists. "Abuela thinks the government is like it was in Germany and Italy forty years ago, during World War II."

"Well, I'm not stupid. La Vieja Zolezzi and I go to a church with other mothers of missing people. The Generals took them away. We want to know what happened to them."

Señor Zolezzi's mother, Rosa Zolezzi, and my Abuela Romanelli came to Argentina after World War II. They had been girlfriends in Italy and were friends for life.

Abuela wasn't through.

"Next Friday we're going to the Plaza de Mayo. We will walk in front of the Pink Palace and demand answers. . . . We decided to carry only bus fare with us because there could be trouble."

I wanted to ask her about what trouble she ex-

pected, but I didn't. Both Mamá and Papá looked uncomfortable, and I didn't want to keep them talking.

At five o'clock Friday afternoon, Abuela and La
Vieja Zolezzi did go to the Plaza de Mayo. Chino and
I went along to watch. The sky was clear with a chilling
afternoon breeze, what we call Argentina sweater
weather.

Fourteen *viejas* walked quietly around the center
monument. Each woman had a white scarf on her
head. Each scarf had a name and birth date sewn in
one corner with light blue thread. The Mothers had
deliberately made their scarves the size and color of
baby diapers and embroidered them with blue thread,
making them the same colors as our national flag.

Each *vieja* carried a picture of her missing person.
They all held signs asking where their children were.

The first half hour nothing happened. Nobody
seemed to notice them. Then, when two policemen
cut through the circle of old women, something did
happen. The police deliberately shoved women aside
as they went through, and one *vieja* fell down. It was
ugly, but she wasn't hurt.

When Abuela got home she said, "It will get worse.
The Generals do not like being questioned."

Three days later soldiers took the *La Opiñon* pub-
lisher away. The Generals didn't like a newspaper asking questions. Mamá was furious. "If newspaper
people are not safe from the army, nobody is safe."

The next week, two van loads of policemen pulled
up at the Plaza and watched the Mothers march

around. They only watched, but nobody missed the Generals' message: If the marches continue the police will take action.

Abuela said they were going to march on Thursdays from then on. "Friday is bad luck. Besides, more people will see us on Thursdays. Our numbers are growing."

She was right; there were often as many as fifty women marching.

The Generals did not back down. They did not want people to speak out. Less than a week later six men wearing dark suits came in green Falcons and stormed into the *Herald*. Mamá got pushed around, hard. One of the *trajes* messed up her desk, pulled out the drawers, and spilled them on the floor. They messed up a lot of desks. Señor Cox, the editor, got arrested and put in jail for thirty-six hours because the *Herald* had reported something a Montonero guerrilla had said in Rome, Italy.

After breakfast the next morning, when our parents left for work, Chichita asked me, "Do you ever get scared?"

"I'm not scared. Why should I be scared? Nobody bothers me, and I don't mess with anybody. I have no reason to be scared."

"Why is Mamá so mad at the army? She used to say they would make things better."

"I don't know, ask her. I don't understand everything she gets mad at."

Chichita was upset. "I did ask her, but she wouldn't talk to me. Told me to get busy with my homework."

She paused a minute. "Does Papá ever talk to you about what is going on? Why men break into the newspaper, why Abuela marches in the Plaza?"

She was right about nobody talking to us. Neither one of our parents told us anything that helped us understand what was happening; they just told us to stay out of trouble. I'd seen for myself what Abuela was doing, but I didn't know what she expected to get out of marching around the Plaza de Mayo.

"*Hermanita*, I don't know what's going on. Papá doesn't say anything to me, either. . . . Tell me what bothers you."

"Sometimes I am afraid walking down the street alone. Have you heard about girls being picked up?"

"A story, Chichita. Somebody is *trying* to scare you. Pay no attention."

"The sisters at school tell us. They say not to get caught alone."

The sound in her voice said it better than the words. She was really frightened, and if the nuns were warning girls, it must be a problem. The sisters see the devil everywhere, but that doesn't mean they make up stories about danger on the street.

I didn't want to worry her even more, and I didn't want to sound like a grown-up telling her not to be concerned. "*Hermanita*, I never heard about girls being taken off the streets, but the sisters must be trying to help. Make sure you are not alone. What else can you do?"

May fifth was the first time the Mothers marched on a Thursday. It was the biggest Mothers' march up until then. Many more people than mothers and grandmothers went to the Plaza de Mayo. Old men, young men, young women, and children marched with them. The Mothers stood out from all the others because they wore the diaper scarves over their heads.

One week later the police started arresting them, and the marchers ran away. Chino and I watched from across the street under the covered sidewalk.

Abuela, La Vieja Zolezzi, and a dozen other women ran to the opposite side of the Plaza and hid inside the National Cathedral. The police tried to go in after them, but the women held the doors shut. The cops stopped pushing the doors and stood there. It looked like all those *viejas* were safe. The police were stopped at the cathedral doors.

A police captain went around behind the church, and one minute later he was back. He said something to a man holding a bullhorn. The bullhorn blared out: "The cardinal has given his approval for the police to go inside the cathedral and arrest the women."

A few minutes later I saw Abuela alongside a cop. He grabbed the back of her coat and pushed her toward a police bus. All the old women were put on the bus, and it drove off.

Mamá was right about people not being safe from the Generals, even old ladies in a church.

I ran all the way to my father's office. I was sure he would know what to do.

He got Abuela Romanelli out of jail after twelve hours. Señora Zolezzi was in for twenty-four hours. Papá was plenty upset about what happened, but he didn't say much. He acted the way I do when Mamá does something I don't like. I get mad first and then a little scared to show it. Mamá thinks I should not get mad at her.

The next morning, at breakfast, Papá told me to come to his office. Whenever my father wanted to talk with me without being bothered it was always in his office, just the two of us, what he called man-to-man talks.

He began by talking about the deed to our new house. "It's been months, and the deed hasn't arrived. I can't figure out why. The government is slow, but not so slow if you pay them. I gave a *coima* to get it processed quickly, but it's still not here. The remodeling won't begin until I get it. Your mother is impatient."

I didn't care. Things were going fine for me.

Then he got to the real reason he wanted to talk to me.

"You found a body in the river?"

I nodded.

"Did you look at it?"

"No more than I had to. I helped get it on the riverbank."

"Did you see any marks on the body?"

"I didn't look. It was swollen and had a yellow shirt. Chino said he saw marks that looked like burns and the feet looked like boiled chicken legs, all white and sort of shriveled."

Papá's face was dark, his eyes squinted, and his mouth was tight. "You answered the police questions, nothing more?"

"*Sí . . .*"

"Told them the truth?"

I nodded.

"Good! Now, about your grandmother's political activity."

"Political activity? *Señor*, I don't know about any political activity. Is it political to ask about a missing person?"

He made a little smile. "This is not a good time for you to learn politics."

"What?"

"Atre, you're not a *muchacho* anymore. You are a *joven*, and young men sometimes act without thinking, are quick to judge right and wrong, get mixed up in bad politics. I wouldn't want that to happen to you."

"Me?"

He made one of those father smiles like when he thinks I'm just a kid. "Probably not you. You're interested in making money, and as long as you stick with that and stay honest you'll be fine."

Then he took in a deep breath like *he* was getting

ready to do a high dive. "Stop going to the Plaza de Mayo for the marches."

I couldn't keep my voice down. "*Señor!* If I hadn't seen Abuela get arrested she might still be in jail. What's wrong with helping?"

His shoulders sagged a little. He looked sad. "I appreciate what you did. But the government does not like what those women are doing. Stay away from them, at least for a while."

I shook my head. "You tell me not to hang around the La Boca hoods and now I can't be around Abuela?"

"Those women are political, Atre. People call them *Las Locas de la Plaza*. Abuela wouldn't want you to get hurt because of her."

"Hurt? What do you mean, hurt? Who is hurt?"

"It is you I'm thinking about, Atre."

He had always said to stay away from troublemakers, and I guess that's what he thought about the Mothers of the Plaza, they were troublemakers.

"How about the police, and the army and navy men who come and get money from you? You're friends with them."

He didn't like my attitude. "That's business. When you run this company you'll do the same. I buy their tickets and donate to their projects. It's good business to have connections in the right places. That doesn't mean they are best friends."

I nodded.

He smiled, but his eyes weren't happy. He gave me a little jab in the ribs. "Believe me, your grandmother will understand."

"Papá, did you know Chichita is scared someone will grab her off the street? Do you know why she thinks that?"

"She is a little girl. She gets mixed up. It's nothing."

"Why is Mamá mad at the government all the time?"

"Your mother is always mad at something. She's like that. Why all the questions?"

"Well, Abuela was in jail, and at school we read newspaper stories about a lot of people missing. People get killed."

Now he *was* worked up. "I told your mother you should not go to that school. Fancy rich kids who think money makes them important."

"And Chino told me the navy dumps bodies in the ocean."

That was it. He exploded. "Has Chino seen bodies being dumped in the ocean? Have you? Has anybody? You better mind your own business, *muchacho*. Stop listening to stories."

He bit his lip like he didn't want to say any more. He put his hand over his eyes a moment before looking at me. Was he trying to hide something? His words came slowly. "It is a Dirty War. The guerrillas have to be stopped. They kill hundreds of innocent people. They want to destroy our country. That is why the army took over. All we can do is go on working. You can study hard. Be a good student. Stay out of trouble. Things will get better."

"*Señor*, some people don't think the army is on our side."

He looked grim. "You keep away from those people. Let grown-ups worry about it."

I was more mixed up than ever. He was scared, and if the army scared my father, it was something to worry about.

9

30 OCTOBER 1976, BUENOS AIRES: A United States Catholic organization has issued a scathing indictment against Argentina for human rights violations. Specific cases include the unexplained reappearance of Patricia Ann Erb at Bella Vista Police Station. Also mentioned were numerous clergy arrests, especially a priest who was recently released from La Plata prison, where he had been held for several months with no charges against him.

FRIDAY IS SUPPOSED TO BE A BAD-LUCK DAY, AND FRIDAY the thirteenth the worst.

Friday, May thirteenth, started out with dark rain clouds and Papá's man-to-man talk. At school, in our Western history class, we talked about a street shooting: a Swedish girl, Dagmar Hagelin, was killed. The army said Dagmar hung around with terrorists.

The newspaper said Dagmar Hagelin was eighteen and she had a Swedish passport. She met a woman at Mar del Plata and played games with the woman's little baby down on the beach. The woman turned out to be a Montonero guerrilla, but Dagmar didn't know it. Government men shot Dagmar down in the street. A green Falcon took her body away.

Señor Lefiel, our teacher, asked what we thought about the story.

I said the girl was killed for playing with the wrong baby.

He asked others what they thought. Howie the Klunk said she was hanging around with guerrillas whether she knew it or not.

Most agreed with me. Even Howie said if Dagmar's father wasn't a diplomat we probably wouldn't know about it.

Dolf Miller, an even bigger jerk than Howie, said Dagmar probably was a terrorist. He said if the police took someone there had to be a good reason. Some people agreed with him.

Dolf and me got in a big argument. We started pushing each other. Then Señor Lefiel broke it up and made us stay after school.

I missed all the regular buses and waited an extra twenty minutes for the next. It hadn't rained yet, but the clouds were still there and they looked heavy.

When I got back to La Boca, about five that afternoon, I turned the corner to our house and got empty-cold inside. Men from our warehouse and some neighbors stood around outside in little groups like at a funeral. A big Peugeot was parked in front. Nobody we know has a Peugeot. When I looked at people they looked away. Whatever had happened, it wasn't good.

Mamá, Chichita, Abuela, Uncle Fredo, Aunt Nina, and La Vieja Zolezzi were all inside.

Chichita was crying. Aunt Nina was crying. I

stopped at the door and looked for Papá to find out what was going on.

"Where's Papá?"

Mamá saw me. I never saw her look so old, her mouth drawn down, eyes bloodshot; the bags underneath were puffed up and almost black. She looked hurt, but more than just hurt. It was an ugly-angry-mad look, not just her regular mad.

Her body was stiff with anger when she hugged me, relaxing only for a second. Her voice was icy flat. "A *patota* took him!"

My brain stopped working. The room got stuffy hot, made me sick to my stomach, and burning vomit rose in my throat. Then, the thought smacked home. I ran to the bathroom.

The suit had heard me tell Chino about Señor Zolezzi! I knew I wasn't supposed to tell anyone about Señor Zolezzi, but I told Chino. The *traje* heard me. Why did I tell? Why take Papá?

I flushed the toilet, wiped my face, and went back to the living room.

Mamá was busy talking to Uncle Fredo. Her sister, Aunt Nina, was married to Uncle Fredo the air force colonel. Fredo had on civilian clothes, and I remembered his air force car wasn't in the street. He must have come in the Peugeot. Why would he drive a Peugeot instead of his air force car?

Feet pounded up the front stairs, and Chino burst in. He was ghost white. "What happened?"

Nobody answered at first. Then Abuela came over

to us and told us what she knew. It was like listening to a school announcement: "Two green Falcons went to the warehouse, and four men in civilian clothes broke into your papá's office. They handcuffed him and took him away. He only had time to yell out, *'Tell Nida!'* . . . Nobody knows what the *trajes* said or why he was taken. The warehouse foreman called your mother, and she came right home."

"Were they police or soldiers?" Chino asked.

"No one knows."

"When did it happen?"

"Two hours ago."

Chino moved toward the door. "I'll go ask Busti if he knows anything and be back in a minute."

I grabbed his arm and whispered, "He heard me tell you about Señor Zolezzi. Maybe he turned Papá in."

Chino nodded and left.

Mamá was on the phone arguing with somebody. She got loud.

"*I* will run the business *until* he comes home."

She listened for a few seconds, then said, "*I* will do this. If I need help, *I will* call you." She banged the phone down.

"You have a lawyer?" Uncle Fredo asked.

"Guillermo Martín is Ricardo's attorney. Why?"

"Get him to file a writ immediately. Make them show Ricardo to you and set bail for his release."

Abuela pushed in. "He will not do anything. Lawyers are afraid to do anything."

Mamá sounded disgusted. "Mu-thurr!"

She never talked that way to Abuela, but Abuela didn't flinch. "You will find out soon enough."

Abuela turned to Uncle Fredo. "Call your brigadier, Fredo. Ask him to find out where Ricardo is."

Uncle Fredo wouldn't look at her.

"Can you not ask him?"

Uncle Fredo didn't say anything. He was always telling everybody what to do, and now he wasn't talking. He wasn't going to do anything.

Mamá was mad. "How brave, Fredo!"

She had the phone again and was dialing Señor Martín.

Abuela spoke up. "Nida, just because he is a colonel in the air force doesn't mean he cannot disappear."

"What is a family for?" Mamá asked.

"Nida?" Uncle Fredo sounded embarrassed. "Please understand. I have my own children to think of."

Mamá didn't say anything, but her face told me what she thought.

Abuela kept talking to Mamá and Uncle Fredo even though Mamá was busy dialing the phone.

"We don't want to get each other in trouble," Abuela said. "It is best if we not call one another on the phone. Someone may be listening."

Mamá gave her the same look as before. "Mu-thurr?"

"Nida, she is right," Uncle Fredo said. "We must be careful . . . at least until we know more. Maybe he will come back."

Chichita and my aunt were still crying. Señora Zolezzi tried to comfort them, but nothing helped. I
wanted to do something for my sister. But what? I
wanted to cry myself. Maybe if I was alone I would
have, but not there, not then. I went over to Chichita
and touched her shoulder so she'd recognize I was
there. She took my hand and held it close to her face
for a long time. She never stopped crying.

The lawyer finally answered, and Mamá said, "Guillermo? This is Nida Romanelli. I need your help. Ricardo was taken." She listened for a long time. My
father's lawyer must have had a lot to say.

At last she said, "Guillermo, I do not give a damn
about excuses. If you expect to make another Romanelli peso, get your butt down to our office in thirty
minutes. I'll be waiting." She slammed the phone
down.

I don't know what surprised me most, Mamá's lan-
guage or how tough she was. Where'd she learned to
talk like that? But it worked. Everybody in the room
treated her differently from that moment on.

She looked at Abuela sitting with Chichita and
walked over. She patted Chichita's head, nodded at
Abuela, and motioned to me to follow her out the
front door. We headed for the warehouse office.

"You are the Romanelli man now, so pay attention."

When we got there, Guillermo Martín was waiting.
Señor Martín looked OK. He didn't seem upset.

The first thing he said was "Don't get the wrong

idea, Señora Romanelli. I'll do whatever I can to help
Ricardo. Try to remember, if I'm in jail I am no good
to him. Do you have any idea how many attorneys are
already in jail for trying to submit writs? . . . Here."
He handed Mamá a piece of paper. "This is the writ
of habeas corpus you need. Give it to Judge Honero,
personally. . . . Now, as you so clearly ordered, my butt
is here. What do you want me to do?"

For the first time since I got home Mamá made a
little smile, but she didn't say she was sorry.

"What do you advise?"

Señor Martín talked about what might happen to
Papá: Maybe it was a temporary arrest. Maybe he'd
made bad friends. Maybe they wanted information
about someone else. Maybe someone in the government was mad at him. The list of possibilities was end-
less.

We already knew what *could* happen. We needed to
know what *had* happened.

"Ricardo told me you have relatives in the United
States. When someone in the States asks for help in
locating someone in Argentina, it gets our government's attention."

"A cousin, yes. Her family has a ranch near Los
Angeles. I send her Christmas cards."

"That's enough. Call her right now. Time is important. The sooner the better."

"What do I tell her?"

"Tell her to send a telegram to her United States
congressman today, saying Ricardo was taken. Tell the

congressman to have the State Department ask the Argentina government about Ricardo. Make certain the name Ricardo Romanelli II and his address are spelled out fully and correctly. The Argentine police will ignore if it there is any way they can. Even the smallest error is enough for them to ignore it. Tell her to call on her congressman in person. Tell her we will pay for all expenses. She may want her own attorney's help. Remember, time is crucial."

Mamá was already on the telephone talking to the international operator. She started giving her the cousin's name and address.

Chino came in the office. "Busti doesn't know anything or else he won't say. You have an idea where they took him?"

"Quién sabe?"

Chino said, "There are four places in the city where they take people."

Señor Martín interrupted. "I have heard of the places myself."

Chino continued, "Atre and me could go to all four and ask them if he is there."

Mamá was trying to listen and talk to the overseas operator at the same time.

"Yes, Operator, Santa Paula, California, eight oh five, five two five, oh oh oh one." She didn't stop, didn't look up. She opened her purse and tossed something to me. "Take this." She threw a roll of *yanqui* bills at me. "We must try everything."

"Hold up a minute," Señor Martín called out. "What will you say? What will you ask?"

I stared at him. I hadn't figured out what I'd say.

"Whatever you say, be serious and do not volunteer any information. As far as you know your father is helping the authorities and has not been able to get in touch with home. Make sure they know that you know the government men took him. You are only asking them to tell you where he is. Understand?"

Chino made a thumbs-up, nodded, and said, *"Claro!"*

Señor Martín added, "Sometimes people are picked up and released after a few hours. In fact, Ricardo could be on his way home right now, so don't panic. . . . And for God's sake be careful!"

10

4 DECEMBER 1976, BUENOS AIRES: Newsman Robert Vacca is missing. Mr. Vacca was supposedly on his way home from television channel seven last night when he disappeared. His last newscast summarized increasing government success in ending the guerrilla war. It included a report of seven left-wing extremists killed in a shooting and the death of Novana Arrostito, chief of the Montonero guerrillas. Mr. Vacca has no record of political involvement.

AN ORANGE SUNSET AND BLACK RAIN CLOUDS GAVE the sky a *Día del Muerto* look as we got out of the cab. Two brawny cops shoved us aside as we went into the downtown Central Police Headquarters.

The desk sergeant made fun of me. "*Muchacho*, don't you know what day it is? Your old man is playing a Friday the thirteenth trick on you. He'll come home. It's a joke."

We didn't leave, and he got angry. "He ran off with his girlfriend. Maybe the guerrillas took him. Now get out of here. I'm busy!"

We were outside waiting for another cab when the drizzle started. All the cabs filled up in a hurry. We stood close to the building to keep from getting soaked.

Chino whispered, "They still got your papa. That sergeant knows it, too. They haven't let him go."

He didn't have to explain why he whispered.

"How do you know?"

"It's the same thing they said about Horsey's old man. Right? They always say the same thing."

"What about Zolezzi?"

"I hear lots of things at La Barca. Sometimes, when I wash dishes, a pair of *trajes* park their Falcon in front and come sit at the back table and drink coffee. If it's not too noisy, I hear them talk through the wall. They don't know I hear."

"What'd they say?"

Chino stepped out from the building a second and looked both ways before stepping back. The whisper never left.

"Not just the *trajes*. I heard three UTP *hombres* talking about a lot of union leaders disappearing during the coup, from lots of different unions. The leaders just disappeared."

Two neighborhood cops came toward the entrance. When they got within ten meters, Chino stopped talking and tried to wave down a cab that was already full. Raindrops sprinkled my face as the rain got stronger.

The policemen hurried inside, and Chino continued. "Later on the *trajes* were laughing about crowding men on a river barge during the coup, called them Commies and Reds. I put one and one together. All the disappeared union leaders didn't run away with girlfriends, that's for sure. No one's heard from any of them."

A taxi stopped in front of the entrance to let an old woman out. We rushed over and jumped in.

Chino leaned toward the driver. "Navy Mechanics' School!"

I looked at him and squinted. "Why are we going to a navy base?"

"It's one of the four places. We'll check the other two on our way back. Don't expect any good news, *amigo*. They're all going to say the same thing."

The rain was pouring down by the time we got to the Navy Mechanics' School. The taxi dropped us at the guard shack and sped away. The sailor on guard duty was a bit older than us, eighteen maybe, with a lot of pimples. But he acted military and stopped us from going in his shack.

Chino tried to push on inside. "*Cuidado, hombre! I'm ruining my shoes out here.*"

The guard looked down at the shiny red Nikes and motioned us to stand under the eaves. He still wouldn't let us in his shack, but at least we were out of the downpour.

The guard didn't know anything, and he wasn't about to let us on the base. But we didn't give up. Finally, he phoned the commander's office and asked about Papá. The commander didn't know anything about Ricardo Romanelli.

"Sorry," the guard said. He sounded like he meant

it. He wasn't so military after all, just one more *joven* doing his year of national service, a conscript. He called us a cab.

It was still raining and by then too late to go on to the other interrogation centers. We went back to La Boca to figure out what to do.

I decided to talk to Busti alone. He was Papá's friend and might tell me something he wouldn't tell Chino, but it was ten o'clock at nighit. I had to wait until morning.

Mamá stopped reading the boxes of papers for a few minutes. She said she'd talked with her cousin in the States for an hour. Then she'd made another call to the United States to someone with Amnesty International. It's an organization that helps find disappeared people. They told her they would start asking the government about Papá.

Mamá also talked with her friends at the *Herald*, told them about Papá, and changed her work hours. She would still work part-time for the newspaper because she felt safer if she kept her job there.

She gave the writ to the judge Señor Martín told her about. Mamá went to the judge's house that afternoon. She said the judge took the writ and shrugged. He looked sort of sad but didn't say anything.

I spent the night thinking about all the hateful things I'd said to Papá, things I wanted to take back. I remembered how I'd embarrassed him with Bustamante, how I'd held out the Caminito money. I never told him about the diving money either. I wondered if the men in the green Falcons knew about me and had taken Papá because of the fake ID cards. I wanted to cry like Chichita, cry out loud, like when you're little and the sound of your crying sometimes makes you feel better. I opened my mouth and tried, but no sound came, only the tears.

After a while I got up and knocked on Chichita's bedroom door.

"Who is it?" Her voice was hoarse and weak from crying.

"Can I come in?"

"Come."

I sat on the edge of her bed and patted her head. I wanted to make her feel better. There wasn't anything to say. I was hurting, too, but maybe not exactly like her. Papá always said she was his little girl. I was never his little boy.

"I'll sit outside your door until you go to sleep. OK? If you want anything you call. OK?"

She nodded.

An hour went by before her soft crying stopped and she was asleep. I went back to my room and don't remember going to sleep that night, but I guess I did 'cause I remember waking up.

The rain stopped sometime during the night. Saturday morning was bright and shiny.

Mamá stayed up all night I guess. The next morning she was still reading Papá's company books. Two more large boxes of papers were on the floor beside her.

From the look of the kitchen sink, I'd say she drank

about a gallon of coffee. Argentine coffee is black as
tar and thick as syrup. It's so strong that if you could
get a gallon of it down a corpse the body might sit up.

Mamá should have looked tired, but she didn't. She
was ready to go.

"I'm going to the office for a few hours and talk to
the workers. I called them in for two hours. We'll pay
them, naturally. I want you with me . . . and when we
finish at the warehouse I'm going to Police Headquarters, the Pink Palace, and both Army and Navy Headquarters to ask about Papá. . . . Do you need anything
before we go?"

I shook my head and told her I wanted to see Officer
Bustamante. She agreed.

Two hundred men and a few women waited for us
at the warehouse.

Mamá stepped up on a pair of cargo pallets so they
could see her. "You know that Señor Romanelli is
missing. I am here to tell you three things: First, business will go on. The superintendent and foremen will
continue to run the daily operation. Second, as of now
I am in charge of this company. If anyone has a problem with working for a woman, tell the bookkeeper
and collect what is coming to you. I hope no one
leaves, but it's your choice. You are *all* needed."

Her voice turned hard as granite. "Third, Ricardo
will be back! We will find him."

There was no discussion. She said what she came to
say, stepped down from the little platform, and headed
straight toward the door. Every eye followed us. The

room was so quiet you could hear us walking. Most tried to make eye contact with Mamá, and those that did nodded. They all stepped back, opening a path to let us pass. Caps and hats came off as we walked to the warehouse door and into the street.

"Ricardo, keep an eye on your sister. Help her and mind your *abuela*. Don't worry, she'll not treat you like a child as long as you are respectful."

She stopped and hugged me real tight. "I count on you, *mijo*. I need your help to stay strong."

"*Sí*, Mamá."

I had never seen her so strong.

11

18 DECEMBER 1976, BUENOS AIRES: *Editorial.* *"Herald* Commends Government Efforts to Stop the Guerrilla War." Still, the war continues. Terrorist bombs killed twenty-three people in the past two days. However, armed assaults and open confrontations with the army and police have all but disappeared. This change in guerrilla tactics signals that the government has taken the upper hand in the struggle.

BUSTAMANTE MUST HAVE AVOIDED ME FOR SOME reason because I couldn't find him until Saturday noon. He was in Gino's Barber Shop Café drinking coffee.

"Atre, I'm sorry about your father. Ricky's been a good friend. I hope he comes back soon. Maybe he'll not be away long." The way he said it sounded honest. He probably was sorry. Still, he wasn't offering help, and he was a cop. He had to know something.

"Busti . . . Señor Bustamante, is there something you can say to me? We don't know why he's gone. Do you know anything?"

He looked right in my eyes and pointed at his sleeve. "These two stripes say I'm a senior neighborhood patrolman, not an officer. I'm not a sergeant, lieutenant, or captain. I'm a policeman. I don't know what goes

on outside my precinct. The officers tell me what I
have to know. That's all."

I sat there without saying anything for a long time.

He fidgeted with his notebook, shrugged his shoulders like his neck hurt, coughed, and signaled Gino.
"Want some coffee?"

I shook my head. He drank the second cup in a
gulp.

Gino walked into the kitchen, leaving me and Bustamante alone together.

Busti spoke in a near whisper. "I don't know what
happened to your father, but meet me outside in a few
minutes. Drink something before you come out.
Don't let anyone think you're following me."

In a louder voice he called, "*Adiós,* Gino. *Gracias*
for the coffee."

Fifteen minutes later I caught up with him as he
walked through the Caminito. He grabbed my arm
and pulled me to the far end of the street and pushed
me up against the wall. There was nobody within hear-
ing distance. He started talking in his regular voice,
but his hands and arms moved around like he was mad
at me. The action didn't match his words. Then I got
it: He wanted everyone to think I was in trouble.

"I told you the truth. I don't know where Ricardo
is." He spun me around to face the wall as he talked.
He patted me down hard; his hands slapped loud on
my body. I felt a hand slide a piece of paper in my
back pocket, and he turned me around again. We were
eyeball to eyeball, with his finger at my nose. His voice

growled low like a big dog's warning. "The names on the paper are four neighborhood cops. They work near the interrogation centers. Show them your father's picture and say, 'Busti is looking for this *vivo*!'. Say it exactly that way and nothing else. Memorize the names and get rid of the paper right away."

He shoved me and walked away to the little monument at the Caminito entrance. He stood there, giving no indication he was going to move.

I stepped out of sight and memorized the names. Then I stepped back where he could see me, wadded up the notepaper, and stuck it in my mouth. It was the biggest spitball I ever ate.

For a second Busti looked like he was going to smile, but he didn't. He turned and headed for the bridge as if nothing had happened.

I practiced the names in my head a thousand times. Finding four strange policemen in a city as big as Buenos Aires would be hard even knowing their neighborhoods. And I still didn't know where two of the interrogation jails were.

I wanted to tell Chino what Busti had said, but I didn't dare tell anyone, not even him. Not only that, I couldn't start looking on my own before Monday. Neighborhood cops don't work Sundays.

That same Saturday afternoon Chino and I went to the other two known interrogation centers. The first one was a government printing office warehouse in San Telmo near the *Herald* building.

If it hadn't been for the green Falcons constantly

coming and going, no one would have suspected what was going on inside. The man in the little front office said we were in the wrong building and chased us away.

The other place was a police station on the western edge of the city. They said the same thing we'd heard the night before: "Your old man must have run off with his girlfriend or the guerrillas got him."

I felt awful. My stomach hurt. I couldn't think straight. I was responsible for Papá being taken away. I knew what I'd done, but I couldn't understand why telling Chino about Señor Zolezzi was so bad.

Chino tried to cheer me up, said we'd find him. He sounded confident, but I knew what he was thinking. I knew Chino almost my whole life, and he couldn't fool me. He didn't believe what he said. He just wanted me to feel better. We got off the west side bus at the Obelisco to catch the La Boca bus.

"Want a pizza? I'll buy!" Chino offered.

"I'm not hungry."

"Your stomach is growling."

He led me to a pizza place we always liked, a place where we'd had lots of fun. The tablecloths were stained, and the forks were bent. I was hungrier than I thought. I drank three large Pepsis, and when the waiter brought my second pizza who should come through the door but Howard Klone, Howie the Klunk.

He smiled big like we were long-lost cousins.

"*Hola, amigos!* Good to see you. Chino, how are you?"

I tried to perk up. No need for Howie to know my business. Besides, Abuela had stressed the point: *Do not tell anyone our problems.*

Howie sat down beside us as if we were three *amigos.* He spoke Spanish, acted like he wanted to be Chino's friend. I guess he still felt bad about when he'd tried to give him a thousand-peso tip.

"Do you know what the Generals are doing now?"

We both shook our heads.

"We have to pay more book tax next term on our textbooks, practically double the price. It's not fair!"

Chino shrugged. He didn't pay for schoolbooks anyway, and he snatched the other books he wanted. "So what? The Generals are always doing something."

Howie puffed up like he had every right to be mad. "It's only us. Public schools get their books free, and church schools don't pay the tax; only the private schools like ours will pay."

"Well, don't pay it. Bookstores know nothing," Chino told him.

Howie leaned over the table. "You get a textbook tax waiver form to give the bookstore, don't you?"

"*Verdad!* So? Hand them anything. They don't look."

The Klunk shook his head. "It has your official school seal signed by the headmaster. They look at that."

This was a dumb conversation. I heard Howie, but who cared? I wanted him to go away. He had started to get up when Chino got bright eyed. "If you had a tax waiver form from my *colegio,* could you get books without the tax?"

Howie sat down and leaned back, considering the idea. "Well, I suppose so. But there's no way . . ."

Chino and Howie kept talking, and I started thinking about my father, glad to be out of their conversation.

12

3 March 1977, Buenos Aires: Argentina Government Blasts United States for Interference. The United States recently cut military aid to Argentina from 36 million dollars to 15 million dollars. The Military Govern- ment issued a strong protest, calling the action, "Meddling in our affairs." One spokesman said, "The U.S. ambassador to Argentina appears to be out of touch with the fact that we are at war."

THAT NIGHT WAS THE SAME AS EVERY OTHER NIGHT. Mamá worked, Chichita cried, Abuela slept, and I stared at the dark and felt more guilty than ever.

Sunday morning is usually quiet, but this morning a racket came from outside. Mamá was yelling at me to come out. I jumped into a sweat suit and hurried to the sidewalk. About forty neighbors stood on the sidewalk, looking at our house.

Graffiti was spray-painted all over the front: Commies, Communists Here, Traitors, Subversives Inside, The Enemy Lives Here, hammers and sickles, swastikas, U.S. dollar signs, and some swear words.

Who could have done it? La Boca people don't do things like that. In La Boca, you got a problem with somebody you might punch their lights out but you don't paint their house. What good is it to be mad and not let the *pendejo* know you're mad?

Mamá looked at the house, looked at me, shook her head, and went inside.

Chichita came outside, groaned loud, and ran back inside with her face in her hands.

Abuela stood and read it. She read without saying anything. She might as well have been reading a book. When she was through I went inside with her.

Half an hour later our doorbell rang. I answered it. Four men from the warehouse stood there with paintbrushes and buckets. One was Jorge, a foreman, and three helpers.

Jorge said, "Your father, uh, that is, your mother has some leftover bottom paint from the *Góndola del Mar*. Do you think blue looks good on a house?"

I got pretty choked up. They'd stuck their necks way out to come help us on Sunday. Any other day it would have looked like a job they were paid to do. Not on Sunday.

I tried to smile. "Blue is our favorite color."

They touched their caps and went to work.

"Who was that at the door?" Mamá asked.

"Neighbors, Mamá."

I stood by the front door and felt hot tears in my eyes. Those men cared about us. It gave me a strange, happy-sad kind of feeling.

Jorge and the other three men finished painting in two hours. We still had time for church.

As soon as Abuela, Chichita, and I got outside, we

all smiled at Mamá, who was obviously happy with the color. If you'd ever heard her complain about living in La Boca, you'd know how funny it was to see her stand there admiring her bright blue house. Bottom paint on houses was one of the things she said she hated most about La Boca. Until that day our house was always pure white.

People left us alone after church. Before then we always talked to lots of people, but not that day, and not on any Sunday for a long time afterward. They were afraid to be seen with us, all except La Vieja Zolezzi and a couple of other old women from the Plaza de Mayo.

The *viejas* looked old and weak, like a strong wind would blow them over.

As we walked home, Abuela talked to me. "The old women know something the others do not know. We fight back. It may take a long time for most of the people to understand how important it is to fight, to stand up to the Generals. Not everyone understands us Mothers of the Plaza, only some. A few people speak against the green Falcons, the *chupaderos*, the *patotas*, the missing, and the torture. It is dangerous to speak out. The list of disappeared gets longer."

Monday I decided not to go to school. I got Papá's photo from a box of family pictures. Then I started looking for the neighborhood policemen Busti had told me about.

All neighborhood cops get free meals and coffee from the cafés on their beats. It was easy enough to ask about them by going to cafés near their precinct headquarters. I'd order a Coke and wait for a busboy to come by. Talking to someone my age was easier than talking to an adult.

I always said I was from another town, just passing through, and Officer So-and-so knew a friend of mine back home. If Officer So-and-so stopped there, what time did he come in? I always finished the drink and left quietly. An unfinished Coke might give someone the idea I was a nosy outsider. I didn't want anyone remembering me.

The first day I found two of the policemen, one in San Telmo and the one downtown. With Papa's picture cupped in my hand, I held it up and said, "Busti is looking for this *vivo*."

The San Telmo cop had slicked-back hair pasted on his head like a tango dancer. He blinked at the picture and looked back at me. "Can't help you, *muchacho*." He walked away.

The next one, the downtown policeman, was scruffy for a neighborhood cop and more relaxed. He reached over and took the photo. His cuffs were worn through. He looked at the picture for several seconds. "You say Busti wants him?"

I nodded.

"What for?"

I didn't know what to say. I shrugged my shoulders and held my hands up.

"Bustamante is your *amigo*?"

"*Sí*, most of the time."

"I don't remember seeing this *vivo*, but I will think about it. Come back in a week."

I got a little dizzy, sort of light-headed. Come back next week meant he might know something.

When I got home that afternoon, Abuela was upset. She said the headmaster had called to ask if I was OK. She stared in my eyes and all over my face. You could practically see the wheels going around in her head. Her face softened, but her voice was strict. "Go to school, Atre!"

That was all she said, no threats, no lecture, no long explanation, nothing about what Mamá would say or how Papá would feel, and no questions. I still didn't feel like going to school.

The next day she gave me a note saying I hadn't been feeling well.

After that she made sure I went to school every day, but my grades dropped anyway. Daily quizzes weren't easy anymore. It was hard to pay attention. I never read the class newspaper articles, didn't talk. I wasn't interested. Señor Lefiel asked me a lot of times if anything was wrong. I said I'd been up late, which wasn't really a lie.

The nights got harder and harder for me. Some nights I barely got to sleep. Over and over the darkness told me I was guilty. Then I got mad, mad at Papá for letting them take him, for getting us in this mess. That made me feel even worse. Wherever he was I knew he wanted to be home.

Every night I talked to Chichita before she went to

bed and sat outside her door until she cried herself to sleep. Mamá worked late every night. She must have taken short naps; nobody can go without sleep forever.

Only Abuela slept well and got up early. She made us get up and eat breakfast. It didn't matter to her how long we slept or didn't sleep. She got us up, and when we left the house she always did something with the Mothers of the Plaza.

Every day after school I tried to find one of the two neighborhood cops I hadn't showed Papá's picture to. I didn't have much time, and it was a long way to the west side of Buenos Aires. Buses were crowded that time of day, smelling of sweaty armpits, dirty smoke, and cheap perfume. We jostled back and forth, side to side, holding on to overhead pipe rails. Sitting was as uncomfortable as standing.

The cop by the Navy Mechanics' School wouldn't even look at Papá's picture.

"Don't know him. Haven't seen anybody. I don't see nothing. I don't think I will see anything." He was so scared I doubt he saw the people on the street.

Thursday afternoons the Mothers met in the Plaza de Mayo at three o'clock. With Papá gone I went along to be close to Abuela and La Vieja Zolezzi. Chino came most Thursdays.

Police always came. They watched. A few marchers got hauled away, and sometimes the police used clubs. When they came out of their vans with their clubs, I'd take Abuela's hand and Chino took the *vieja*'s. I pushed anybody and everybody who got in our way.

"Hurry! Get across the street. Hold on. Walk fast."

The cops didn't care who they hit. Every time the police beat up old women, the crowd would be smaller the next week. They even stopped going to the Plaza for three weeks, but then they were back.

Chino worked at La Barca most afternoons. He said school took a lot of time. We saw each other a couple evenings a week at Gino's. Saturdays, whenever Mamá or Abuela had me deliver messages to the lawyer, notes to Amnesty International, or big brown envelopes from the La Boca Mothers of the Plaza group to another group, Chino went with me.

We always stopped at the pizza place, where the flash of hot air and the smell of warm cheese when an oven opened always made me hungry and got me thinking about food.

Most times we ran into Howie there. Chino actually started liking him.

"How did a stone head like you ever get into *Rose-ah-belda*?" he asked Howie.

Howie giggled and tried to punch Chino's arm to show he was a regular guy, but it didn't quite work. Howie was a klunk. He punched sort of floppy wristed. But he loved the attention.

He started talking about the next semester's book tax one more time, and Chino told him to shut up.

"Klunker! You got enough money to buy a book factory, so stop complaining about a little tax. Talk about *fútbol*."

"Actually, I don't know a great deal about *fútbol*,"

Howie answered, "but I am a good chess player. Do you play chess?"

"I'll give you a queen and a bishop and still kick your dumb *yanqui* ass," Chino told him.

Howie could hardly wait to play chess. He invited Chino to his house. They may not have been the only two guys in town wearing red Nike running shoes, but when they were together you couldn't miss them.

It took weeks to find the downtown policeman a second time. He said he might have seen my father going into the Central Station, but he wasn't sure. He remembered it as the same day Papá disappeared. And he might have seen Papá the next day in a backseat leaving the underground garage.

It wasn't much to go on, but it was something.

The minute Mamá heard about it, we went back to the police and the army and navy headquarters. She was always polite and wouldn't give up. We waited hours to see people. They all knew her.

Army headquarters was like all the others. We waited three hours to talk with a major, who might talk to the colonel, who would consider talking to the general, who sometimes talked to the police.

The major's office was spotless. He sat in a tall leather swivel chair that kept swinging from one side to the other while he sipped coffee from a big brown mug.

"We know you have him," Mamá said. "Your men took him. He was seen in your custody. Where is he?"

"You are a very busy woman, *Señora*. Managing a business and working for a newspaper at the same time."

"Please, Major, just tell us where he is. What has he done?"

"Your newspaper does not appreciate us. We are making Argentina safe for the people."

"My husband does the same thing. He creates jobs, pays wages, gives to your charities."

"Why does not the *Herald* print the whole story? Señora Romanelli, you should talk to your editors."

"Major, I am a copy translator. The editors do not ask my opinions. However, they do want to know where your green Falcons take the missing people."

"*Señora,* I am busy. We know nothing about your husband."

They never knew anything about Papá, but they stopped talking about girlfriends and guerrillas.

Before my father was taken away, Mamá and Chichita had been looking forward to moving, Papá was waiting for our new house deed to arrive, school was good, and me and Chino had plenty of money for pizza, parties, and fun. All that changed overnight.

"No one calls anymore," Chichita complained. "I used to get many calls. Why is it that no one calls? Even our family does not call."

"Stop complaining and do your homework," Abuela told her.

Mamá also talked about the silence. "Señora Rodriguez and Señora Bonino met me on the street yesterday and wouldn't stop. They smiled and kept walking. I've know them for fifteen years, and they were never too busy before."

That was the way it was. All the neighbors smiled nicely, but they didn't have time to talk. The silence was awful.

Roosevelt School asked Mamá to come and talk about me. Naturally she didn't tell them what was wrong. She tried to make them think it was only temporary. She was sure I would do better. I was barely passing.

Chichita left the house every morning like she was going to school, but she didn't go. The nuns talked to Mamá. Mamá talked to Chichita. Nothing changed.

Then I tried. "Chichita, I don't feel like going to school either, but I go."

She folded her arms. "You go and sit. If you don't study, why go to school?"

"I know I'm not doing so good, but at least Mamá knows where I am. You can do that. She has enough worries."

She stopped listening. There isn't a lot you can do with a person if she wants to sneak around.

Chino's Santa Maria Colegio is across the street from Chichita's school, the Santa Clara Secundaria for Girls. He said he'd keep an eye out for her.

Life went on that way all though May and June. I looked forward to the July break, when I'd have more time to look for Papá.

13

5 March 1977, Buenos Aires: *Editorial.* "Violence and Reality." In two days time, 69 writs of habeas corpus were filed, two journalists disappeared, and one business executive was kidnapped and murdered. This isn't even the full catalogue of horrors we have come to look upon as normal. We must ask: How far have we come since last March twenty-fourth? The guerrilla war is finished and peace is as far away as ever.

T HE THURSDAY AFTERNOON BEFORE WINTER BREAK began, Chino saw Chichita smoking cigarettes with Horsey Zolezzi at a place near our warehouse. Friday afternoon I learned about Zolezzi and my sister. The next morning I walked past the warehouse and toward the place Chino had told me about. A block away, Horsey and Chichita sat on a pile of broken pallets, smoking.

Chino joined up with me at the warehouse corner. *"Cómo te va?"* he said.

"Going good."

"You don't look like things are going so good."

"They'll get better, you watch."

"Oh, I am. I'm watching. You think the *gorila* is going to be a nice boy likc those at *Rose-ah-belda*? This is Horsey Zolezzi; he doesn't know enough words to fight like a gentleman. He has a muscle where you have your brain. You're on his ground. There are no *hombres* here interested in keeping this fight fair."

We were almost close enough for them to hear. Chichita threw her cigarette in the river and turned her back toward me. Horsey had an ugly smile. He couldn't wait for a battle to start.

"I know he's an animal. It doesn't matter."

"What will you hit him with? An insult?"

I wanted Chino to shut up, but I didn't want him to leave. If Horsey really got to beating me up, Chino would do something.

"Fists, feet, elbows, knees, I'll do what I have to."

"Atre, we're in La Boca, remember? What it takes is a club. *Por Dios,* pick up a club."

We stopped in front of the pallet pile.

"*Hermana,* come on home."

She still wouldn't look at me.

"Come home, Chichita. It isn't good to hang around the river."

She turned around a little, but she still wasn't looking at me.

Horsey started in like I knew he would. "Go away, Ree-Car-Dough! I'll take care of her."

I stepped closer to him. "This is my sister, Hector."

Horsey stood up and looked down at me. He had grown a lot more than I had in the last year. His fists tightened.

"She's your sister." His voice mocked me. "Does big bad brother want to hurt sister's boyfriend?"

He started to grab me. I was ready, but he stopped cold. Chino was tapping him on the shoulder with a piece of pallet wood the size of a baseball bat.

Horsey turned toward Chino. The pallet board was drawn back ready to swing. If he let go, it would take Horsey's head off.

Chino was very calm. "Let him take his sister home, Hector. This is family business."

Horsey stood riveted in place; his eyes flicked first at me then at Chino. "Two on one, huh?"

"Trying to make it even, Hector."

Chichita stepped down beside me. "I'll go home."

"Stay here!" Horsey ordered.

Chino said, "Horsey, don't do this. If anyone can understand what is happening here, it's you. Your families are a lot alike."

The fight ended before it started. No one said it was over, but everybody knew it. Chichita and Chino walked away with me.

Horsey called out, "Hey, Stick! I'll remember this. I'm not through with you."

Chino threw the club back on the pallet pile without answering.

I nudged him. "He means it this time, *amigo*. You better watch him."

Chino nodded. He knew Horsey was serious.

"What are you going to tell Mamá and Abuela?" Chichita asked.

"That I bought you a Pepsi at Gino's to make you feel good. That is what I'll say, but it isn't the reason

I'm buying you a Pepsi. I don't want Mamá or Abuela smelling your cigarette smell. When we get to Gino's, go wash your hands and face, get the stink off."

She didn't argue. In fact she seemed to feel better than she had in quite a while. She sort of pranced along between Chino and me.

"Anyway, I'm not going back to school."

"You'll convince Abuela you're sick?"

"What are you talking about?"

"If you don't go to school, you have to stay home. You can't walk around La Boca all day."

"No one cares."

Chino stopped her. "Can't you see who cares?"

"Who will stop me?"

"Your brother or me if you make us."

Chichita began teasing him. "Roberto Echavarria! Would you tell on me? I am your almost sister."

He put a fake scowl on his face and lowered his voice: "Do fish eat worms?"

We all laughed. It was just a little moment, but we all felt good for a minute.

I wish that had ended it. Chichita went back to school only so far as being inside the building. She skipped classes and wandered the halls. She was always helping a janitor or a clerk, anything to stay out of class. The nuns kept Mamá informed and showed a lot of patience, but there was no way they would let it go on forever.

Winter break began July fifteenth. Mamá sent Chichita to a convent in the Recoleta district. She lived in the convent and worked with the sisters. Mamá told her, "You decide for yourself if you want to stay in the convent, where you don't have to go to school. Or you can come home and act right. It's up to you."

Mamá also had new orders for me: "Bring your schoolbooks home. Every morning you will sit in the warehouse office and read until you catch up. The afternoons belong to you."

My mouth opened to say something, and she cut me off. "We all have work to do. Maybe we don't feel like it. Maybe it isn't our best work. But we try! We try as much as we can."

Every morning I looked at pages, turned pages, tried to read, pretended to read. Sometimes I actually read. Reading was the same whether in school or the warehouse. I wanted to feel like reading. I wanted the good feeling that comes after you study hard, get frustrated, and then catch on. I used to like it, but the feeling didn't come back.

After one week Mamá and Abuela visited Chichita in the convent. They came home surprised.

Abuela said, "God's will, Nida. It's for the best. She is happy in the convent. That is why she wants to stay."

Mamá was still sad. "She barely talks. Her eyes are empty."

"The sisters care for her, Nida. They look after her and are good to her. We can see her anytime. Let her find peace in work."

"It's grubby work," Mamá snapped.

"It is work," Abuela answered. "She is busy. That is enough for now."

14

9 MARCH 1977, BUENOS AIRES: *Editorial*. "Human Rights and Wrongs." Who is violating human rights in Argentina? It is clear to everyone that the war against the subversive left is being won, but how about the subversive right? Senator Yrigayen had the courage to speak out against right-wing terrorists and he is in jail. Why? We have maintained a conspiracy of silence, but now the human rights question is in the open.

ONE NEWSPAPER STORY WAS SO WEIRD IT WAS LIKE something out of the last century: "Generals Challenge *Herald* Editor to Duel." The headline wasn't in the comics, but I still read it twice to make sure it was a real news story. It actually happened.

Three retired generals and one admiral went to a lunch meeting with some ex-Nazis. The newspaper reported it and said the military ought to watch out who they hung around with, or words like that. All four of those old goats wanted to fight a duel. Dueling is illegal, but they were serious.

The editor chose his weapons, boxing gloves. He offered to meet them one at a time in a fight ring with gloves on. That ended it. Even those old crackpots knew they couldn't get it on in a fistfight.

• • •

Our company worked harder than ever. We didn't have a single business slump. The money came in as expected, so nobody was trying to cheat Mamá—at least they weren't cheating any more than before. My father always said, "Remember, someone is always trying to take more than his share. Just don't let him take too much."

After ten mornings in the warehouse office, I understood what Mamá was doing. She kept two phones going all the time. Talked business on one phone and searched for Papá on the other.

More than fifty letters went to the government from outside Argentina asking about my father. Relatives in the States, Italy, and Germany wrote letters. Government offices in those countries wrote letters. Boat and ship builders in the States, Japan, and Singapore wrote letters. Argentine politicians wrote letters. Amnesty International asked about the missing practically every day. The letters always had the same basic message: Where is he? You took him. We know you took him, now we want him back.

The letters didn't come by magic. It took work to get every one. People outside Argentina couldn't believe anything like the Disappeared could happen.

Neither could I. I came home from school one day and my father was gone. He isn't dead, he isn't alive. Not killed in a car accident, not missing in action like a soldier. He wasn't killed as an innocent bystander;

not in the wrong place at the wrong time. He didn't run away. He was taken in a government automobile by men nobody knew and simply "disappeared."

Mamá spent hours explaining the importance of each letter, where to send it, and describing the Dirty War to anyone who would listen. A lot of people said they were sorry but didn't want to get involved.

Five afternoons a week I made the rounds of government offices asking for Papá. They never knew anything about him, but they knew we were not going away. They knew that I would be back, that others would come asking the same question, over and over. They knew we knew they had him.

Chino went with me sometimes but not always because he was working on a vacation art project, something with wood blocks that I didn't pay any attention to. He threw a blanket over them when I opened the door one day and immediately started talking. "We should go back to the Navy Mechanics' School and try to make friends with the gate guard with all the *granos*."

I was skeptical about wasting time on a gate guard. "What for? He's only a conscript sailor."

"*Verdad,* a poor sailor, and he probably hates the navy the same way all conscripts hate the service, especially now. He's like us, maybe a year or two older, and he might like friendly civilians for a change. Don't forget, he sees who goes in and out of the navy school, and according to what I've heard, it's the biggest interrogation center in the country. *Comprende?*"

Yes, I understood. It couldn't hurt. So far we had not one military person helping us in any way. Uncle Fredo could have moved to outer space for all we saw of him. One teenage conscript sailor wasn't much, but it was better than nothing.

"The *trajes* were talking about moving prisoners from prison to prison, especially those with many people looking for them. If Granos keeps his eyes open, maybe he will see your father."

We waited a half block from the gate guard shack until he came on duty. Then we went over and started talking to him. He remembered Chino's red shoes and the fuss he'd made about getting them wet.

It turned out that Chino was right about the pimply-faced sailor: he hated the navy, missed his friends, and didn't like the way civilians treated sailors. He had six weeks left before his year of national service ended, and he was counting the days.

Granos hesitated about saying anything at first. We asked when he got off, told him we'd come back, maybe go get a pizza, Cokes, Pepsis, beer, whatever. We said we wanted to know what the navy was like 'cause we both had conscript duty coming up and we had experience on ships.

Granos's father was a *gaucho* on the pampas, and that was what he wanted to be, too. He didn't like the city and didn't like city people. He was homesick. One summer on the *Góndola del Mar* was enough to make me understand how he felt.

After two or three pizzas we got along fine. He hadn't seen anyone who looked like my father because he made it a point not to look in the Falcons' backseats when the *trajes* drove in and out. He looked at Papá's photo and said he would look for him but it wouldn't be easy. The *trajes* got upset if anyone, even gate guards, got curious.

Winter break was coming to an end, and time was running out. I made at least seven trips to the west side of town without finding Officer Colorado. He was the last one on the list Bustamante had given me.

School started August first. Howie the Klunk wasn't there, and I guessed he was sick. Neither was Señor Lefiel. He had said he was going to the States on vacation and showed us his travel ticket. He must have been held up by a late plane or something. The headmaster took over his class.

I noticed that Señor Lefiel's bookcase was almost empty. He usually kept maybe fifty history books in there. We borrowed them overnight sometimes but not over vacations. He wouldn't have taken them with him. At the end of the day I asked a janitor if he knew what happened to them. He said two men came and got them.

"Teachers?"

"*Profesores?* No. *Dos hombres* in a green Falcon."

I remembered the censor had a thing about books and figured he was doing his stupid book-burning act.

I still had enough time left that day for one more trip to the west side.

The cabdriver dropped me at a café two blocks from the West Side Police Headquarters. My watch read four-forty-five. The busboy I usually talked to wasn't anywhere I could see, so I sat down at a back table and ordered a Pepsi. Five minutes later two men in dark suits came in, walking directly toward me.

The first man's voice was brassy. "Come with us!"

"What for?" I know my voice sounded innocent. I was innocent.

In a flash I was dangling thirty centimeters above the floor, gripped by a pair of very large hands. When the hands slammed me down, my feet stung. Before I knew it I was handcuffed and being shoved out the door, then stuffed in the backseat of a green Falcon like a laundry bag.

I was alone, lying on the floor in the backseat, smelling somebody's stale urine. I coughed. Gravel and dirt ground into my face. How could this be happening?

It was worse than any nightmare. It was the end of my life. I didn't think about anything except not wanting to die. The picture of a man facing a firing squad flashed in my mind. He hears "*Ready . . .*" and knows he is ten seconds from dying. The clock in my head went crazy. One minute felt like one hour. An hour felt like a minute. I lost track of time altogether. It could have been a day, a week, a month, I don't know.

I struggled to sit up on the car seat far enough to peek out the window. The *trajes* ignored me.

I know they took me to the West Side precinct because when we drove in I recognized the garage door. The little room they put me in had two metal chairs with a tub of water between them. They jammed me onto one chair. I didn't say anything. I couldn't think of anything.

"Get undressed!" one ordered as the other took off the handcuffs.

"Undress? I should take my clothes off?"

"Everything, shorts, socks, everything."

It was cold sitting naked on a metal chair.

The man put the handcuffs back on, this time behind my back.

The other one put a cloth sack over my head, and I couldn't see.

I heard the door open and the shuffle of feet on the cement floor. It sounded like two people might have left and maybe two or three others came in. The door clicked shut.

It was quiet for a long time. I wanted somebody to say something.

"Who's there?"

Nobody spoke.

An hour or a minute later another man's voice said, "You are Ricardo Romanelli. What business do you have out here? You do not live here."

The voice was firm and even, not angry, the sound of someone with a lot of patience.

It was hard get my mouth working. My voice squeaked. "I am looking for my papa."

Splash! A rock-hard hand grabbed the back of my neck and shoved my head underwater. Only the summer swimming kept me from drowning. When the hand let go, I was coughing and my nose was plugged up.

"You belong in La Boca. Your father does not do business out here."

"He is missing. I look for him."

"Did your father tell you to join the rebellion?"

"I don't understand."

Water ran down my forehead into my eyes. My throat was dry.

Splash! Again my head was underwater. This time for much longer. My lungs were about to burst wide open when the hand let go.

The firm, even voice went on. "You and your friends make a conspiracy."

"No! No! What is it?"

"You and your *amigos* tried to defraud the government."

"Defrog the government? What does *defrog* mean?"

Two hard, tiny knobs touched my lower back.

Zap!

Zap-Zap!

Zap-Zap-Zap!

Three times crippling pangs shot through my legs to the bottoms of my feet and all the way up to my head. Electric shocks jolted my body out of control. I was helpless. I screamed, I cried, and it stopped.

"Was it your idea or one of your friends'?"

"Sir, *Señor*, Mister, I don't know what you mean."

Zap-Zap!

Somebody screamed. I was completely paralyzed, and the blood sizzled inside my arms and legs. It was me screaming.

"*Por favor, Señor*. Please. I know nothing. What do you want me to say?"

Zap-Zap-Zap!

This time the pain started in my crotch. Warm urine splattered my legs, and I heard it drip on the floor.

"Tell me the truth."

He was so calm, and I hurt so much. It was the worst thing, ever.

"I will tell! I will tell!"

It was quiet a second or a week or . . .

A branding iron touched the back of my hand, I smelled myself burning, opened my mouth to scream, and threw up in my lap. Then everything went black.

I woke up a minute later, ten seconds later.

"Was it your plan?"

"*Señor, por favor, Señor!* Help me. Help me. I will tell you everything, honest."

The electric shocks had left me weak, my skin trembled, but the pain stopped. My branded hand kept on hurting.

"You and your friends plotted against the government. You planned to protest the government's new actions. Did you say the government is unfair to private schools?"

I tried to think. I remembered something. What was it?

"*Señor*, I did. I did. I'm trying to remember. Give me a second. I will tell . . ."

My mind raced backward. Where was it? Who was it? What was it? The sour Pepsi smell rose from my lap to my nose. Pepsi? It came back to me: Taxes!

"*Sí, sí*, the book tax!" The voice was squeaky and loud. It came from somebody else, but they were my words.

"Howie talked about the book tax. I wanted him to go away. I didn't do anything. I don't know any more. I do not know any more. I do not."

I began crying and couldn't stop.

For a minute or a day it was quiet again, and the firm, even voice said, "Yes! . . . We know all about it!"

The door scraped open. Feet shuffled out. The door clicked shut.

15

5 July 1977, Buenos Aires: *Editorial.* "No Other Solution?" Argentina's human rights record is questioned throughout the western world. We have no action regarding the Disappeared and no one defends the government against the pro-Nazi charges leveled against it. The *Herald* lauds U.S. Ambassador, Carla Hills, as she continues to press the government to act. Inaction is no solution to human rights reform.

A POLICEMAN CAME IN AND REMOVED MY HANDcuffs. He tossed a wet sponge at me, and I wiped off the filth. When he gave me my clothes, I read the name tag on his jacket: Colorado. I had finally met him.

The burn on the back of my left hand was the same round shape as the holes on the man in the yellow shirt, cigarette size.

A red electric cattle prod lay on the floor by my chair. Two tiny bumps on one end told me it was what had made the pain on my back. The policeman picked it up and leaned it against the wall.

"Do not tell anyone about this evening . . ."

I shook my head. My brain was so numb I barely understood what he said, but I forced my eyes to look at him and tried to understand what he was saying.

"Not your family. Not your friends. No one. Understand?"

I nodded.

"Speak up!" he yelled.

"No sir! No sir! I will not tell!"

"Where did you get the burn on your hand?"

He knew how I got burned. Why ask me that? He knew that. Was he testing me? I had to think of something!

"On the bus. From a cigarette."

"Smoking's not allowed on buses!"

"I know! I know!"

Now, what could I say? All the buses have No Smoking signs. Wait a second, some people smoke on buses . . .

I shouted, *"Some smoke anyway."*

He made an ugly face and nodded. I finished dressing, and he gave me a Band-Aid.

"Qué hora es?" Why did I ask such a stupid question? Who cared what time it was? I was still alive, and it was a good time no matter what time it was.

He didn't answer but motioned me to follow him. We went to the garage. Another green Falcon waited at the door. He pointed, and I got in the backseat. I was alone again in the back of another green Falcon with the same stale smell.

My head still didn't work right. If anyone had asked me to tell what happened I couldn't have said anything. My skin felt creepy, and my arms trembled. My hand burned something awful, and I couldn't think. The Band-Aid helped because it kept air off the burn.

Two different *trajes* drove me downtown. Black building shadows and yellow streetlights swirled in front of my face as we sped down wide crosstown streets. The clock in my brain was still haywire. I only know it was sometime later when the car stopped in an unlit alley. The suit on the right side reached back and opened the car door. He snapped off the one word, *"Vete!"*

The building height told me I was somewhere downtown. I stumbled to the alley entrance, stepped into the middle of the street, and looked up at the horizon, searching for anything familiar. Bright lights lit up a night cloud hovering above a large round dome. I was one block from the capitol building. Without my watch I didn't know the time. The only thing they'd left me was my national identification card; everything else was gone: my money, my school watch, my pen, even my handkerchief.

The capitol is ten kilometers from La Boca, and I didn't feel like walking. I wanted to lie down in a doorway and rest, but I knew better. I struggled to make even that simple decision and began walking.

Four blocks later a bank clock flashed the time and temperature. It was 6:30 P.M., 10 degrees C. It had to be later than that.

I tried to remember when I left school. Wasn't that sometime after four? Got to the West Side, when? I remembered looking at my watch when it was quarter to five. The *trajes* came and got me about five. My God! The whole thing had taken less than an hour.

The school sweater didn't keep me warm. I kept close to buildings, trying to hold off the wind. My feet stumbled on small cracks, and the cold got colder. I huddled in darkened doorways and crevices between buildings to get warm. Many stores were open, but I didn't go in. I didn't want to be seen.

Not until I was halfway to La Boca did my mind work well enough to remember we have telephones. But I quickly rejected the idea of calling home. I talked to myself: You still can't think straight, and you're not even sure of the number. Just keep going, you'll get there.

Officer Colorado's warning echoed in the back of my head: "Do not tell anyone! Do not tell anyone! Do not tell anyone!"

The La Boca bridge lights made fuzzy red balls in the night fog. My head was much clearer after having walked ten kilometers, and my legs were no longer rubbery. I tried to put all memory of the interrogation out of my mind. I could not remember what I had said or what anyone had said to me, only how calm that voice was. I will never forget the pain, but there is no way to describe it. The burn on my hand throbbed, but the intense pain of being branded was over.

When I made the last turn onto our street, people filled the sidewalk coming and going. It wasn't like La Boca families to be out walking at night. Several strange cars were parked on the street. The fancy Peugeot was here again. My eyes traced the line of people. It went directly to my house, up the front steps, and through the open door. All the house lights were on. A lady in the doorway was carrying a covered bowl. Then I saw that many people carried baskets and covered bowls. La Vieja Zolezzi stood in the doorway directing traffic.

My heart stopped beating, and my stomach froze as I raced up the steps.

The house was full of neighbors. They jabbered away, laughed, made jokes. Women hugged, and men nudged each other with elbows and shoulders.

The first person I recognized was Uncle Fredo in his air force uniform. Abuela sat on the couch with Chichita. My grandmother's eyes were red from crying, but she smiled a little smile. Chichita's face was blank, giving no indication of how she felt.

Mamá came out of the kitchen. Her face looked like my sister's. She saw me. If I looked any different, she didn't notice. We hugged, and she felt soft. For the first time in months she spoke in the velvety voice I grew up listening to. "Ricardo, your father is in jail. Isn't that wonderful?"

The cold feeling left, and memories of my family filled my head. I remembered being very small, standing with Papá and Mamá by the clothes dryer. Mamá handed me my flannel pajamas hot from the dryer. I put them against my face to feel the warmth and smell the freshness, laughing because it was something new and felt good. That was how I felt when I learned Papá was alive, only this time I didn't laugh. I felt grateful, that's all. I was amazed to hear he was alive, yet I had never thought he was dead.

Mamá turned away to talk with someone. Everything sort of blurred. I was there and not there. Something was missing. I heard and didn't hear. Uncle Fredo came over, smiling, "Coti Martinez Prison list . . . no charges . . . this afternoon . . . no release date . . . Amnesty called . . . visitors allowed . . . You are going to see him tomorrow."

Chichita took my good hand when I sat down next to her and held on to it. She used to hold it the same way when I walked her to kindergarten. I leaned my head back against the soft couch and went to sleep.

I woke up screaming. All the neighbors and relatives were gone. Mamá was holding me.

"You had a bad dream. It is over now. Go to bed. We must leave here at one o'clock tomorrow."

It was dark in my room, and I didn't want to be in the dark, so I left the light on. I lay down on the bed and closed my eyes.

Mamá said, "Do you want the light off?"

I put my hand over my face and shook my head. She started to close the door, but I asked her not to. I was remembering the nightmare, the calm voice, the water, electric pains, being burned, Colorado's warning.

"Yes, we know all about it," the voice said.

All about what? What did he know about?

Chino yelled, "Run, Atre! Get away. Go! Use my Nikes. . . . Run!"

Then another voice, "Amnesty called . . . Coti Martinez Prison list . . . visitors allowed . . . yes, we know all about it . . . no charges . . . we know all about it."

Chino again: "It is a long way down. I don't know, Atre. I don't like high places . . . Run! Get away! Use my Nikes."

I sat straight up in bed. *Chino wasn't here tonight!* That was what was missing. The one person I knew would be here, and he wasn't. And Howard Klone hadn't been in school today.

16

16 JULY 1977, BUENOS AIRES: *Editorial.* "San Martín's Warning." Argentina's founder left his country and returned to Europe a discouraged man. He warned us of the dangers in maintaining weak institutions, especially the press. This nation owes a debt of gratitude to the opposition politicians who understand San Martín's warning. Many have been jailed, several kidnapped, and some are among the Disappeared. The *Herald* congratulates them for their courage.

RIVERBOAT ENGINES SNORTED AND POPPED AS THEY started the day and woke me up early. It hadn't been until morning that I fell asleep. I sat up, shook my head, and tried to think.

If the *trajes* had let me go, they must have let Howie go, too. It was only the first day of the semester; nobody had a book list yet. Even if he had worked out some way to beat the book tax, we always got our books on the second day. Besides, he'd never mentioned it after that one day in the pizza café. Still, the voice knew something! Who could have told him?

I couldn't think anymore. My mind stopped working altogether and I slept.

Two hours later (or two minutes) Mamá woke me. "Señor Echavarria is here to see you . . ."

She grabbed my burned hand, and I flinched. The bandage was gone.

"What happened to your hand? Have you been smoking?"

"No." I tried to remember what was I supposed to say and couldn't. "You know I don't smoke. Let me put on my clothes."

I felt like six shore boats were banging against the inside walls of my head. I needed more sleep. I didn't want to argue. What could Señor Echavarria want?

In that instant I came wide awake. The only thing Señor Echavarria would ever want from me had to be about Chino.

I scrambled to the living room, pulling jeans up with one hand and trying to get the other in the sleeve of my shirt. The ship's clock in the front hallway rang eight bells. It was either eight in the morning or noon. It had to be noon. Chino's father had never gotten up before midafternoon in his entire life.

Señor Echavarria stood by the door wearing a fresh apron and a chef's hat. For the first time in weeks he was clean shaven, but the white parts of his eyes were masses of red lines. His voice croaked with the roughness caused by too much alcohol. "Atre, have you seen Roberto?"

"No, *Señor,* he didn't come here. I'm wondering where he is myself."

"He was washing dishes at the restaurant yesterday afternoon when he got a phone call. Then he hurried out yelling he had to go. I thought he would be here."

"No sir, I haven't seen him. *Señor,* do you know who called him?"

"The cashier said it was a *muchacho* on the phone."

"A *muchacho*'s or a *joven*'s voice? Did she say?"

"She said *muchacho.* . . . Roberto never stays out all night. He is always asleep when I come home."

Once more the words sounded inside my head: *Yes, we know all about it.* I tried putting the pieces together again. *What* did they know? Yes! It was about the book tax! They knew about Howie's protest over the book tax. Could they have heard him talking? We were eating pizza. I hadn't seen any police, and there were no *trajes* in there. I didn't think he ever mentioned it again. Besides, what did it have to do with me and Chino?

Howie had said it was unfair because only private school students paid the tax, and I remember Chino said something like, So what? Then he asked Howie if he could use a tax waiver form from his *colegio.* And I stopped listening.

"Chino is always home when I come in," Señor Echavarria continued, "except when he stays at your house or is gone for the summer. He always lets me know if he isn't coming home. I am very strict about that."

"*Señor,* did Chino ever talk about Howard Klone? Or Howie Klone?"

"*Sí,* the chess player, the one he calls Stone Brain. He came to our place sometimes. Chino might be at his house, no?"

Panic hit me. I took several deep breaths to clear my mind. Chino and Howie had been up to something, and they'd kept me out of it. I couldn't believe it, but if it had to do with money, Chino would have been interested.

"If you don't mind, Señor Echavarria, I'll walk home with you. I think I left something in Chino's room. Don't worry, *Señor*, we'll find him. He may be home now."

I told Mamá I would be back in a few minutes. I had less than forty minutes to go to Chino's and get home. A rented limousine was coming to take us to Coti Martinez Prison in La Plata.

New green and gray ink bottles in Chino's art supply cabinet told me what I didn't want to know. I looked in his trash box and found three small wood blocks with smooth vinyl glued to one side. All three were the size of a textbook tax waiver form. I held them up to the basin mirror to read. Chino had forged the waiver forms for Howie.

The work was incredible. Chino had carved such sharp, even edges in the vinyl that the copies would look like they came from a three-color printing press.

The green one read "Santa Rosa Belda Colegio." The address underneath was different, but the Roosevelt School phone number was on it, very tiny, but it was there. A perfectly etched school seal was in the lower-right corner and looked as official as a passport stamp. Chino probably used the real phone number in case someone at a bookstore called the school. He

must have figured it wasn't very likely anyone at a
bookstore would call the school, but even if someone
did he wouldn't expect them to pay any attention to
whether someone answered *Rose-ah-belda* or Roosevelt.

The gray block was amazing, a soft-tone background print of our school. Only the name was
changed and a crucifix added. Chino had really learned
wood-block printing.

The final block was stamped on top of the gray
school drawing. It was black and had all the regular
printing found on a tax waiver form: Date_____
Term_____Grade_____Number of books_____.
The signature line read, "Fr. Echeveste, Headmaster."

Chino hadn't gone to all this trouble for one copy.
Somewhere he or Howie had a stack of these things,
and they were planning to sell them. Chino was making money, and Howard was still fighting the Generals. Howie must have talked to someone at school.
Somebody heard him and told the police. That had to
be it.

I grabbed the blocks, inks, and scrap paper and
dumped them in the slop barrel behind the restaurant.
If the *trajes* wanted to hunt through slop, let them,
but they were much too proud of their fancy suits to
do that.

I hurried home feeling real torn up inside. We were
going to visit Papá and I wanted to see him, but I had
to find Chino.

The limousine was late. That gave me a few extra

minutes, so I looked up Klone's phone number in my school directory.

The *moza*'s voice answered. "Klone residence."

"Is Howi— Howard there? This is his friend Atre, Ricardo Romanelli."

The maid's voice stopped, and an older woman came on the phone. It sounded like his mother. "Howard isn't here, Atre. He and his brother are on a trip." She sounded funny, sort of stiff, as if somebody was listening to her and she didn't want them to hear what she said. But what she said did explain why Howie wasn't in school. I relaxed a little. Maybe I had let my imagination run away.

"When will he be back, *Señora*?"

The way she answered said she didn't want to talk to me. "He is going to go to school in the United States. Good-bye, Atre."

I yelled into the mouthpiece, "Did he say anything about Chino?" But the phone clicked and a dial tone buzzed at me.

17

22 JULY 1977, BUENOS AIRES: *Editorial*. "Which Argentina Will Todman See?" The United States undersecretary of state visits Argentina tomorrow. What exactly will he be shown and what will he see for himself? The official tour will no doubt focus on the government's success in driving out the Communist inspired guerrilla forces and our growing need for economic aid. What will he learn of the Disappeared, or of the eleven lawyers and wives kidnapped in Mar del Plata ten days ago?

L A PLATA WAS ONCE A CITY FOR RICH PEOPLE, BUT that was a long time ago. Now it is dusty and dirty, with mostly poor people. It is better than a shantytown but much worse than La Boca.

La Plata's Coti Martinez Prison is a one-hour drive from Buenos Aires. The prison's ugly stone walls have barbed-wire tops. My skin crawled just looking at it.

We were allowed to see my father, one person at a time, for only five minutes. Mamá went in first and came out with her face buried in her handkerchief.

Abuela was next. She came out looking happy and very relieved.

I nodded at Chichita, and she went in. She came back crying, but I couldn't tell if she was happy or sad.

The visiting room had a tiny square-top table in the

middle, barely big enough for two people. Metal folding chairs were on either side of the table, facing each other. Three uniformed guards were in the room. They had no clubs and no guns. Papá sat in the chair facing the door where I came in. I noticed he had on high white socks and no shoes. One guard pointed at the empty chair, and I sat down.

I reached out with my burned hand to touch my father, and a guard stepped forward. I jerked back, quickly.

Papá was pale, almost paper white. His face was thin, and he had several little shaving cuts. His hair had been trimmed recently. It looked as if someone put a bowl on his head to decide which hair to leave and which part to cut.

He sat up straight and stiff. Even the slighest body movement showed in his eyes. He looked at the burn on my hand. "Are you well, Atre?"

"*Sí, Señor*. And you?"

"You burned your hand."

"An accident, Papá."

"Yes. I have seen many accidents like yours. But you are well now?"

"*Sí*, Papá. . . . How are you, Papá? When can you come home?"

"I am just as you see me. I am very happy to see you, Atre. Do you study hard?"

I looked away. "Not so hard."

"Try, Atre. Do your best. Promise?"

"*Sí, Señor*. I will. . . . Do you come home, soon?"

Then he did something unusual. He looked squarely in my eyes, and naturally I tried to look away to show my respect. But he called my name, "Atre!" and I looked at his eyes.

"You have seen our new house?"

"Yes, Papá."

"When the paper comes, tell your mother to sell it."

A guard stepped over and touched my shoulder. "Time is up!"

Was it five minutes already? It didn't feel like five minutes. At the door I turned around for one more look at my father. His expression never changed the whole time we were together. Then I looked at his white socks and realized he wasn't wearing white socks. His feet looked like the feet on the man in the yellow shirt, like they had been cooked.

Once back in the limousine, we were all very quiet for a long time. Finally, Abuela sighed. "He is alive, a miracle, but I never stopped believing. . . . He is thin."

Mamá crossed herself. "He is alive, that is all that matters. Now we must let everyone know and ask them to help us get him out of jail."

"When is Papá coming home?" Chichita asked.

I interrupted. "Papá said to tell you that you must sell the new house."

"Yes, I know," Mamá answered. Her face was flat as pavement.

"Why did he say that?"

Her expression never changed. "It is why he is in jail. Someone must want the house."

Chichita stiffened. "Our *new* house?"

There was another long silence before Mamá spoke. "Chichita, we must sell the house before he comes home."

"It is nothing," Abuela said.

"*Sí, es nada,*" Mamá answered.

Late-afternoon fog blanketed La Boca, and the limousine windshield wipers squeaked. The western sun pushed through the soft haze. It lit up our house to a bright blue. In an hour or so the street lamps would come on and turn our street candlelight yellow. The air was cold and damp on my face as I jumped out of the car and hurried to La Barca Restaurant. Chino had not come home.

Señor Echavarria said, "The *trajes* came to my house and went through Chino's room. I do not think they took anything."

Maybe they didn't take anything from his room, but I figured they must have him. Papá's disappearance had taught me that time is important, and my mind raced over what I could do. If I could find him soon enough, if I could find out where he was, or even if I could prove he was taken, there was still a chance to get him back.

I found Busti at the bus stop.

"It doesn't look good, Atre. I saw a green Falcon

parked behind La Barca and figured something was up, but I don't know any more than that."

I jogged down the Caminito hoping to find somebody who could tell me something. All I knew was Chino got a phone call around four-thirty yesterday afternoon and left La Barca. Somebody must have seen him.

Horsey slouched against the back side of the Caminito statue smoking a cigarette. "Hey! Ree-Car-Dough, the Stick is in trouble, huh?" His voice was the same, but the smirk he always wore was gone.

"I think the *trajes* might have him, Hector."

"I know they do. I saw him running toward your house yesterday, and a green Falcon stopped him. They took him."

"Is that all? Did you hear anything?"

"No, I didn't hear anything, but I saw him go away in the car. *Lo siento,* Atre. He was a pain in the ass, but nobody wants . . ." He hesitated. "I am glad to hear your old man is in jail."

I nodded and walked away.

"Suerte!" Horsey called after me.

My heart weighed a ton. In my whole life I had never wanted to cry more than at that moment, and I could not. It was even hard to keep moving, but I could not cry.

As soon as I opened the front door, Mamá asked what was wrong.

"They got Chino" was all I said.

After almost three months of being like steel, Mamá

broke into loud, wailing sobs. I watched her for a long time, head down on the arm of the sofa, crying a funeral cry. She was so strong and now she sobbed.

When my father was taken she never cried, didn't show one tear until we found out he was in jail, and then only because she was happy. When we saw Papá in jail she was still strong. No one was ever so tough and stubborn as Mamá when she could fight. But when she heard about Chino, her fighting temper was all gone.

Why is it that something bad always comes after something good? The *turista* business was going good, and we got caught. We got Horsey's forty *yanqui* dollars, and I found a dead man in a yellow shirt. Abuela was arrested but she got out of jail without being hurt, and then Papá disappeared. Now Papá was alive and Chino was missing.

I was confused and sick when they took my father, but I never thought he was gone forever. Mamá had fought like a tiger to make the Generals give him up, and she was winning.

Who would fight for Chino? He had no relatives in the States. Who would write letters for him? His school would ask about him, but they wouldn't be able to make the Generals pay attention. Señor Echavarria was helpless. Amnesty International would add his name to the list of the Disappeared, but there were thousands on the list.

Chino had me, that was all, and I had caused his disappearance. Because of me he knew Howard Klone

. . . and Howie was going to go to school in the United States.

Because the suit might have heard me talking about Señor Zolezzi, I felt responsible for Papá being taken.

But this time I knew it was my fault. My best friend was gone because of me. I hadn't paid attention. If I'd listened to that dumb plan of theirs, I could have stopped them.

Jerks like Howard Klone never know they're jerks until trouble hits them in the face. Chino should have known, should have read Howie better, but he always thought having money made people smart. Could he have wanted money that bad? Did he really think he could get away with it?

Mamá sat up for a moment and tried to stop crying.

"Mamá, I'm going to the Navy Mechanics' School. There's a guard there. He'll be on duty now. He may know something."

She nodded, opened her purse, and handed me money for taxi fare.

The river fog lifted within two blocks of La Boca. Multicolored lights and neon signs lit up downtown Buenos Aires, and then the fog returned when the cab closed in on the Navy Mechanics' School.

The taxi stopped a block away. My pulse must have quickened because I felt a tightness in my chest. I pushed the night-light button on my electric dress-up watch. It was fifteen minutes until eight. Granos was getting off duty just as I walked to the guard shack. He saw me and immediately motioned for me to move away and keep moving. For a second he held his hand to his mouth like he was taking a bite of pizza and nodded down the street.

Nearly an hour later his grim face came into the pizza café where Chino and I had met him before. He was wearing civilian clothes. The faded jeans, wool poncho, and wide-brimmed black hat made him look like he'd left a horse outside. We sat in a back booth where no one could listen in and ordered Pepsi.

"Chino is *desaparecido*."

His head shook slowly, deliberately. "I was afraid he might be when I saw you tonight."

"You also think something happened to him?"

"Maybe. I can't say for certain. I do know the *chupaderos* were very busy yesterday. I was on the morning watch, eight to noon, and three green Falcons came in early, one right after the other. The people in the backseats were *joven*, at least two were."

"I thought you didn't look in backseats."

"I don't, but even in a half second you can tell the difference between school uniforms and regular clothes."

"And?"

"I saw two *jovenes* who wore the same colors as your school. Green sweaters and gray pants."

"And?"

"Two hours later another car came with a *joven* who might have been Chino."

My heart pumped hard, and my breath shortened. "Why Chino?"

"He wore a blue sweater."

"Many schools wear blue sweaters. Did you see more?"

"I saw the shoes."

An image of red Nikes flashed in my head. Eight million people live in Buenos Aires, and I only knew of one other pair, Howie's . . .

I told myself it was somebody else. It could have been someone else. Nike must make thousands of red and white running shoes. Buenos Aires alone must have hundreds of red Nike shoes. Or maybe it was Howie wearing a blue sweater. He had to have a blue sweater. He could have had five blue sweaters . . . and his mother might have lied to me. Lots of people lied about relatives disappearing.

"Is that why you think it was Chino, the red shoes? Is there anything more?"

"*Sí, poquito más.* That *joven* kicked the wire screen between the back and front seat until he had practically kicked a hole in it."

Suddenly I felt drained. Chino hated fighting. He always tried to stay out of fights, but when he couldn't avoid one he never gave up.

Granos interrupted my thoughts. "Atre, there is something else." He looked at his watch. "It is eight-fifteen. At eight-thirty a friend will talk to us in front of the Córdoba Cinema. He knows more."

I started to get up. "We better hurry."

"*Cuidado!* He will not let you see his face or know his name."

"Why?"

"He is in the navy, like me. We live in the same barracks."

"So?"

"He works on the helicopters."

Images of the long helicopters with rotors swirling at each end popped into my head.

"Why should he talk to me?"

"He is my friend from a village near our *estancia*. We came to the navy at the same time. We will be out at the same time, very soon. I told him about you and Chino, that you are my friends, that you are good *hombres*. You can call *mi amigo* N.N. It is not his name, but call him that, anyway."

"A strange name."

"*N.N.* is the mark put on graves of the unknown dead. It means *No Nombre*."

The Córdoba was two blocks from the pizza café on a brilliantly lighted pedestrians only street with movie houses, restaurants, discos, and small shops, all open until late at night. Hot buttered popcorn, sweet sugar cakes, and charcoal broiled beef smells mixed with the damp night air.

We turned onto the street and bumped past a mass of shoppers and moviegoers, loudmouthed show barkers looking for customers, young couples looking for a place to go, teenagers looking for excitement, and poor people selling lottery tickets. The street was filled with people from noon until midnight, perfect for a private conversation.

Granos stopped me just before we reached the Córdoba. He pointed to a narrow wall extension separating the Córdoba from a record shop next door. It gave me and N.N. a place to talk without seeing each other. I stood on the shop side of the wall, and Granos nodded to someone on the opposite side. Granos was in the middle, facing both me and N.N.

"Atre, say hello."

"*Hola*, N.N."

A whispered voice said, "*Hola*, Atre."

"You two talk, and I will watch for police and the *patotas*. Tell Atre what you saw."

Granos turned around, and N.N. began talking.

"My job is loading helicopters. Sometimes I go along. Yesterday, about five o'clock, I went on a flight to Mar del Plata. Two *trajes* and four prisoners went with us. One of the prisoners might have been your friend."

"Do you know what Chino looks like?"

"No, but it would not matter. The prisoners never look like regular people. Three were hurt so much they were carried to the helicopter and thrown onboard like sandbags. They are always bound with heavy tape."

"What makes you think one of them was Chino?"

"I didn't know any of them. Mothers couldn't tell who many of them are. The one standing up wore red running shoes with white stripes. The shoes were almost new. Granos told me about the shoes."

"Stripes? Not a Nike slash?"

"Maybe stripes, maybe slash. I didn't see them for very long. A ground crew chief pointed to the shoes and looked at the *trajes*. One *traje* nodded back, and as soon as the *hombre* was in the helicopter the chief pulled them off for himself. It was over in a second."

"He was alive when you saw him?"

The whisper voice coughed. There was a long pause before the whisper spoke again. "They went in the ocean."

Chino had told me about the open-door flights. Bodies falling into the ocean. Oh God! Not Chino.

Something stuck in my throat, and my voice choked. "Tell me about it. I have to know. Please."

"We were way out over the ocean when the *trajes* told me to get busy. That means I am not supposed to watch what they do. So I went to a far end of the cargo bay where I could still see them, but they don't know that. . . .

"The first three bodies were slid out the door. The first one might have been dead already, the next two were alive but couldn't move. The last one never gave up.

"He kept pulling away when they touched him, not easy to handle. The *trajes* were very mad with him. They had wide tape over his mouth and eyes, and more tape around his knees and his wrists. They stood him up and took the tape off his eyes. . . .

"He might have been fifteen years, or he could have

been twenty-five. Hard to tell the way his face was. He was skinny with dark hair, like most of us.

"They untaped his legs and the *hombre* held out his wrists like a boxer getting his gloves tied just before stepping into the ring, as if this was a regular thing. He was getting ready for a high dive. The *trajes* looked at each other and shrugged. One of them undid the hands, and the other pushed the *hombre* out the door. . . .

"We were flying at 250 meters, a long way down. That is all I know."

I don't remember anything else, not saying good-bye to Granos or thank you. I don't even remember going home. The next thing I do remember is sitting beside Mamá on the couch.

I must have been talking to her, talking like sleep-walking, telling her what I'd heard, because she asked, "Do you believe Chino is the one the sailor was talking about?"

Mamá's question forced me to think. If I believed N.N., I would have to believe Chino was dead. My ears grew warm; my face must have been red, too. A big angry feeling came inside me, and it got bigger. I doubled both fists and wanted to hit something.

"No!" I shouted. *"No! No! No!* He is not dead. *I do not* believe he is dead. I will *not* kill him!"

Abuela heard me shouting and shuffled into the room in her robe and slippers. She sat down beside me, took my head in her arms, and patted my shoulder. *"Sí, nieto.* We must believe."

18

13 DECEMBER 1977, BUENOS AIRES: *Editorial.* "What Is This All About?" The police deny any knowledge of the disappearance of Señora Azucena from the Plaza de Mayo. Just another Mad Woman of the Plaza, they say. However, she was seen being taken away by police officers in an unmarked Falcon sedan. Her friends report that Mrs. Azucena was responsible for collecting the money for and co-signing a newspaper ad in *La Nacion* that asked the government about the Disappeared. Between eleven and twenty-five other signatories were also taken from outside Holy Cross Church.

FOUR MONTHS LATER THE MOTHERS OF THE PLAZA published a full-page ad in *La Prensa* signed by 237 mothers. Their ad read: "We do not ask for anything more than the truth." Those words reminded Argentina of what President General Videla had said the year before: "Nobody who tells the truth will suffer reprisals."

The Generals did not answer the Mothers' ad.

Two weeks after the ad appeared, hundreds of women demonstrated in front of Congress to present a petition signed by 24,000 people. That was October 15, 1977, the day the Dirty War started coming to an end. But the Dirty War did not officially end until

1983, six years later, when the Generals stepped down and an elected president took office.

President General Videla always said what the Generals did was all right except a few soldiers got carried away. He said there had been "excesses." The Generals admitted that more than 10,000 people had disappeared. The people of Argentina say it was closer to 30,000.

The Mothers and Grandmothers of the Plaza continue the Thursday marches in the Plaza de Mayo.

Howard Klone's parents moved out of Buenos Aires, and I don't know what ever happened to Howie. Señor Lefiel didn't come back either.

Mamá sold the Mar del Plata house to the first person who offered to buy it, an army colonel. He called the same day she put it up for sale. Papá got out of jail right after that.

A policeman lived in our house for a year to keep track of what we were doing. My father wasn't allowed to leave our yard.

The rest of us went on working. Mamá worked part-time at her newspaper job and was the official head of our company. Chichita returned to school, but she worked weekends and vacations at the convent. She liked working there. Abuela worked more and more for the Mothers of the Plaza. A policeman's club broke her wrist, and she went to jail again, this time for two days, but she didn't quit.

When I went back to school, I didn't study harder just to keep a promise. In fact, I forgot I'd made it. I studied for a selfish reason. It blocked out my other thoughts. I can't concentrate on two things at the same time, so for me hard work pushes out the hurt. As long as I work hard I can live with myself.

A photography shop made an enlargement of Chino from my Tonga-Fiji photo. They sealed it in clear plastic and put it on a neck chain. I wear it Thursday afternoons when Abuela and I march in the Plaza.

Epilogue

ATRE AND CHINO ARE FICTITIOUS, BUT THEIR STORY is real. The Argentine Dirty War happened. The events are based on actual occurrences. The newspaper reports come directly from the *Buenos Aires Herald*.

In 1979, the police violence toward the Mothers of the Plaza increased. Finally, it became so great that they had to give up their marches. They continued meeting in churches, pretending to pray while handing around notes.

In August of 1979, Madres de Plaza de Mayo became a legally registered organization and received both financial and moral support from abroad, especially from the Netherlands. In December the Mothers decided they would return to the Plaza in 1980 and withstand whatever the police did to them, even if it meant being killed.

At 3:00 P.M. on January 3, 1980, the Mothers marched for forty minutes. The police were surprised. A week later, the police waited for the Mothers, some even hiding in trees. Several women were beaten and some women disappeared, but the tide had turned. The Mothers never again left the Plaza to the authorities.

From the beginning, the military government assumed that absolute terror would keep people from complaining. They also believed that parents who did not share their children's political opinions would not speak out when their children were taken. The Mothers of the Plaza disproved both of these assumptions.

For many Argentines the Dirty War is not over, and it won't be until their question is answered: "They were alive when you took them. What did you do with them?"

Glossary of Spanish Words and Phrases

abuela—grandmother

adiós—good-bye

amigo—friend

barcazas—shore boats

Belgrano—district within Buenos Aires

cálmate—calm yourself, take it easy

caminito—little street

cinco dedos—five fingers

chupaderos—from the word *suck;* police who arrest large numbers of people at one time suck them up like objects in a vacuum cleaner.

claro—clear (why, of course)

codo—cheap

coima—bribe

colegio—high school

cómo le va? or **cómo te va?**—how's it going?

cómo no?—why not?

compadre—pal, friend, companion

comprende—understand

cuidado—careful

desparecido—disappeared

Día del Muerto—Day of the Dead (resembles Halloween)

dos hombres—two men

es nada—it's nothing

estancia—ranch

estúpido—stupid

fútbol—football, refers to what Americans call soccer

focas—seals

gaucho—cowboy

***Góndola del Mar**—Gondola of the Sea*

gorila—gorilla, thug

gracias—thank you

granos—pimples

guerrilla—rebel soldier

hermana—sister

hermanita—little sister

hola—hello

hombre—man

indios—indians

inflación—inflation

jonnie—British man

joven—young, young man, teenagers

ladrón—thief

La Prensa—*The Press* (newspaper in Buenos Aires)

La Opiñon—*The Opinion* (newspaper in Buenos Aires)

Las Locas de la Plaza—The Crazy Women of the Plaza

lobos marinos—sea lions

loco—crazy, insane

lo siento—I'm sorry

maté—green herb tea

mi—my

mierda—muck, filth (profanity = shit)

mija—my daughter

mijo—my son

moza—maid, waitress, servant

mozo—handyman, waiter, servant

muchacho—boy

muchachos—children

nieto—grandson

niños—babies

no nombre—no name

nunca más—never again

Obelisco—monument in downtown Buenos Aires

pampas—flat cattle country west and south of Buenos Aires

patota—arresting squad

pendejo—pubic hair (slang = creep)

peso—Argentine money

poquito más—a little more

Por Dios!—Oh God!

por favor—please

profesores—professors

que bueno—that's good

qué hora es?—what time is it?

quién sabe?—who knows?

Reservado Turismo—Reserved for Tours

rojo—red, readhead

secundaria—junior high school

señor—sir, Mr.

señora—ma'am, Mrs.

sí—yes

socialistas—socialists

suerte—luck

trajes—suits (slang = government men)

turista—tourist

vale—OK, correct

verdad—true, the truth

vete—go away, beat it

vieja—old woman

vivo—con man